This book belongs to

....

37 Utterly Silly Stories

Compiled by Vic Parker

Miles
Kelly

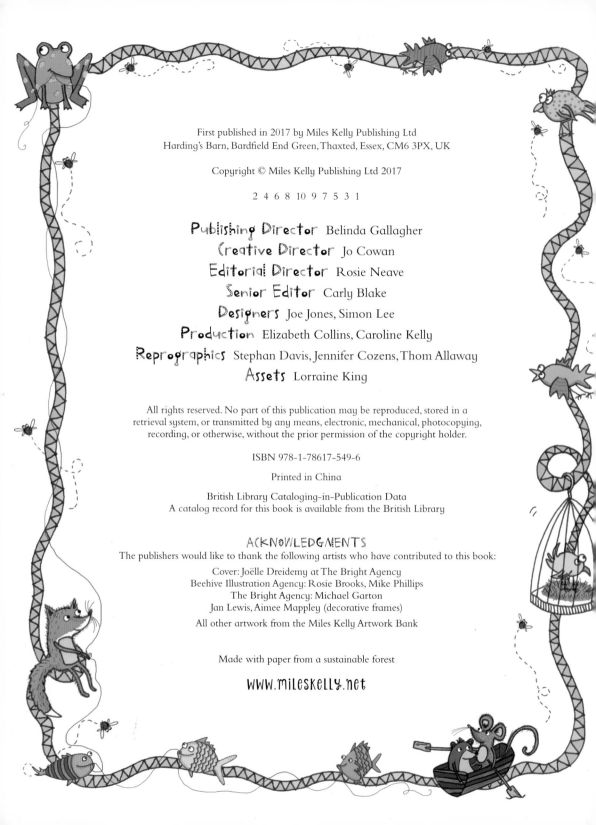

First published in 2017 by Miles Kelly Publishing Ltd
Harding's Barn, Bardfield End Green, Thaxted, Essex, CM6 3PX, UK

2 4 6 8 10 9 7 5 3 1

Publishing Director Belinda Gallagher
Creative Director Jo Cowan
Editorial Director Rosie Neave
Senior Editor Carly Blake
Designers Joe Jones, Simon Lee
Production Elizabeth Collins, Caroline Kelly
Reprographics Stephan Davis, Jennifer Cozens, Thom Allaway
Assets Lorraine King

ISBN 978-1-78617-549-6

Printed in China

British Library Cataloging-in-Publication Data
A catalog record for this book is available from the British Library

ACKNOWLEDGMENTS
The publishers would like to thank the following artists who have contributed to this book:
Cover: Joëlle Dreidemy at The Bright Agency
Beehive Illustration Agency: Rosie Brooks, Mike Phillips
The Bright Agency: Michael Garton
Jan Lewis, Aimee Mappley (decorative frames)
All other artwork from the Miles Kelly Artwork Bank

Made with paper from a sustainable forest

www.mileskelly.net

CONTENTS

Nonsense and Gobbledegook

Tricks and Tomfoolery

Sillies and Simpletons

Baffled Beasts
and
Bamboozled Birds

Nonsense
and
Gobbledegook

Down the Rabbit-Hole

An extract from *Alice's Adventures in Wonderland*
by Lewis Carroll

Alice was beginning to get very tired of sitting by her sister on the bank, and of having nothing to do. Once or twice she had peeped into the book her sister was reading, but it had no pictures or conversations in it. 'And what is the use of a book,' thought Alice, 'without pictures or conversation?'

So she was considering (as well as she

could, for the hot day made her feel very sleepy and stupid) whether the pleasure of making a daisy-chain would be worth the trouble of getting up and picking the daisies, when suddenly a White Rabbit with pink eyes ran close by her.

There was nothing so *very* remarkable in that. Nor did Alice think it so *very* much out of the way to hear the Rabbit say to itself, "Oh dear! Oh dear! I shall be late!" (When she thought it over afterward, it occurred to her that she ought to have wondered at this, but at the time it all seemed quite natural.) When the Rabbit actually *took a watch out of its waistcoat-pocket*, looked at it, and then hurried on, Alice started to her feet, for it flashed across her mind that she had never seen a rabbit with either a waistcoat-pocket or a watch to take out of it. Burning with curiosity, she ran across the field after it, and fortunately was just in time to see it pop down a large rabbit-hole under the hedge.

In another moment down went Alice after it. The rabbit-hole went straight on like a tunnel for some way, and then dipped suddenly down, so that Alice had not a moment to think about stopping herself before she found herself falling down a well.

First, she tried to look down and make out what she was coming to, but it was too dark to see anything. Then she looked at the sides of the well, and noticed that they were filled with cupboards and bookshelves. Here and there she saw maps and pictures

hung upon pegs. She took down a jar from
one of the shelves as she passed. It was
labeled ORANGE MARMALADE, but to her
great disappointment it was empty. She did
not like to drop the jar for fear of killing
somebody, so managed to put it into one of
the cupboards as she fell past it.

'Well!' thought Alice to herself. 'After
such a fall as this, I shall think nothing of
tumbling down stairs! How brave they'll all
think me at home! Why, I wouldn't say
anything about it, even if I fell off the top of
the house!' (Which was very likely true.)

Down, down, down. Would the fall *never*
come to an end? "I wonder how many
miles I've fallen by this time?" she said
aloud. "I must be getting somewhere near

the center of the earth. Let me see, that would be four thousand miles down, I think…" (For, you see, Alice had learned several things of this sort in her lessons in the schoolroom, and though this was not a *very* good opportunity for showing off her knowledge, as there was no one to listen to her, still it was good practice to say it over.) "Yes, that's about the right distance—but then I wonder what latitude or longitude I've got to?" (Alice had no idea what latitude was, or longitude either, but thought they were nice grand words to say.)

Presently she began again. "I wonder if I shall fall right *through* the earth! How funny it'll seem to come out among the people that walk with their heads downward! But I shall have to ask them what the name of the country is, you know. Please, Ma'am, is this New Zealand or Australia?" (And she tried to curtsy as she spoke—fancy *curtsying* as you're falling through the air! Do you think you could manage it?) "And what an ignorant little girl she'll think me for asking! No, it'll never do to ask, but perhaps I shall see it written up somewhere."

Down, down, down. There was nothing else to do, so Alice soon began talking again. "Dinah'll miss me very much tonight, I should think!" (Dinah was the cat.) "I hope they'll remember her saucer of milk at teatime. Dinah my dear! I wish you were down here with me! There are no mice in the air, I'm afraid, but you might catch a bat, and that's very like a mouse, you know. But do cats eat bats, I wonder?"

Alice began to get rather sleepy, and went on saying to herself, in a dreamy sort of way, "Do cats eat bats?" and sometimes, "Do bats eat cats?" (For, you see, as she couldn't answer either question, it didn't much matter which way she put it.)

She felt that she was dozing off, and had just begun to dream that she was walking hand in hand with Dinah, and saying to her very earnestly, "Now, Dinah, tell me the truth: did you ever eat a bat?" when suddenly, *thump! thump!* Down she came upon a heap of sticks and dry leaves, and the fall was over.

Alice was not a bit hurt, and she jumped

up on to her feet in a moment. She looked
up, but it was all dark overhead. Before her
was another long passage, and the White
Rabbit was still in sight, hurrying down it.
There was not a moment to be lost: away
went Alice like the wind, and was just in
time to hear it say, as it turned a
corner, "Oh my ears
and whiskers, how
late it's getting!"

She was close
behind it when
she turned the
corner, but the
Rabbit was no
longer to be
seen. She found

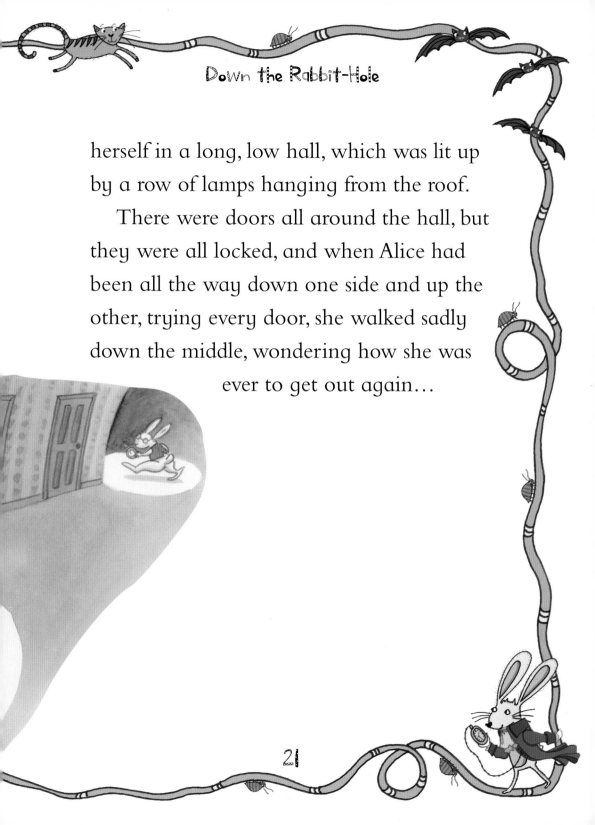

herself in a long, low hall, which was lit up by a row of lamps hanging from the roof.

There were doors all around the hall, but they were all locked, and when Alice had been all the way down one side and up the other, trying every door, she walked sadly down the middle, wondering how she was ever to get out again…

The Four Little Children Who Went Round the World

By Edward Lear

Once upon a time, a long while ago, there were four little people whose names were Violet, Slingsby, Guy, and Lionel, and they all thought they should like to see the world. So they bought a large boat to sail round the world by sea, planning to come back on the other side by land. The boat

was painted blue with green spots, and the
sail was yellow with red stripes. When they
set off, they only took a small Cat to steer
and look after the boat, besides an elderly
Quangle Wangle, who had to cook the
dinner and make the tea, for which they
took a large kettle.

For the first ten days they sailed on
beautifully, and found plenty to eat as there
were lots of fish. They had only to take
them out of the sea with a long spoon,
when the Quangle Wangle cooked them,
and the Pussy Cat was fed with the bones.

During the daytime, Violet chiefly
occupied herself in putting salt water into a
churn, while her three brothers churned it
violently, in the hope that it would turn into

butter, which it seldom—if
ever—did. In the evening they
all settled into the tea kettle,
where they all managed to
sleep very comfortably, while
Pussy and the Quangle Wangle
managed the boat.

After a time, they saw some land at a
distance, and when they came to it they
found it was an island made of water quite
surrounded by earth. It was perfectly
beautiful, and contained only a single tree,
five hundred and three feet high.

When they had landed, they walked
about, but found, to their great surprise,
that the island was quite full of veal
cutlets and chocolate drops, and

The Four Little Children Who Went Round the World

nothing else. So they all climbed up the single high tree to discover, if possible, if there were any people. Having remained on the top of the tree for a week, and not seeing anybody, they concluded that there were no inhabitants. When they came down, they loaded the boat with two thousand veal cutlets and a million chocolate drops, and these kept them going for more than a month as they voyaged onward.

After this they came to a shore where there were no less than sixty-five great red parrots with blue tails, sitting on a rail in a row, and all fast asleep.

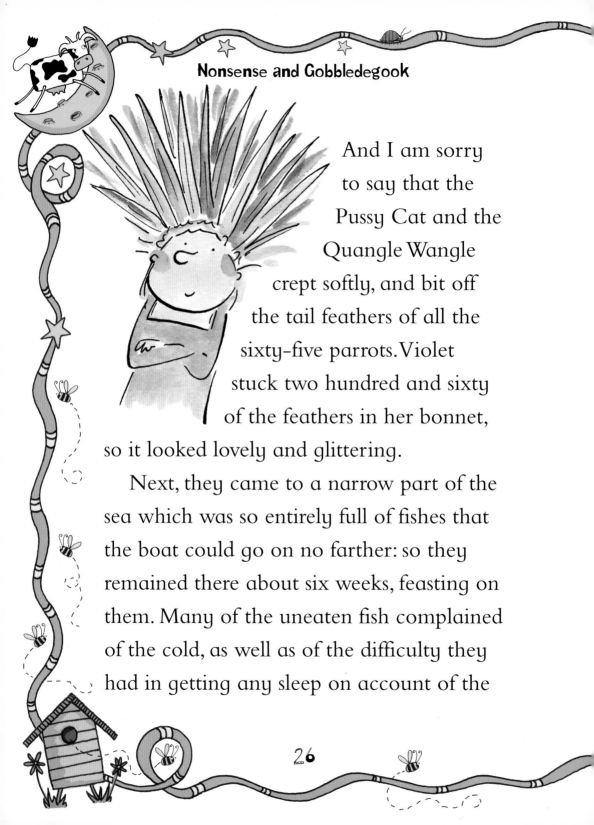

And I am sorry
to say that the
Pussy Cat and the
Quangle Wangle
crept softly, and bit off
the tail feathers of all the
sixty-five parrots. Violet
stuck two hundred and sixty
of the feathers in her bonnet,
so it looked lovely and glittering.

Next, they came to a narrow part of the
sea which was so entirely full of fishes that
the boat could go on no farther: so they
remained there about six weeks, feasting on
them. Many of the uneaten fish complained
of the cold, as well as of the difficulty they
had in getting any sleep on account of the

extreme noise made by the neighboring
Arctic bears, so Violet knitted small woollen
frocks for them. Then they were quite warm
and slept soundly.

Next, they came to a country that was
covered with immense orange trees, quite
full of fruit. So they all landed, taking with
them the tea kettle, intending to gather
some of the oranges in it. But a most
dreadfully high wind rose, and the oranges
fell down on their heads by millions and
millions. They thumped and bumped them
all so seriously, that they were obliged to
run as hard as they could for their lives.
Besides, the sound of the oranges rattling on
the tea kettle was terrifying!

They got safely to the boat and, after

sailing on calmly for several more days, they came to another country, where they were pleased and surprised to see countless white Mice with red eyes, all sitting in a great circle, slowly eating custard pudding.

As the four travelers were rather hungry, tired of eating fish and oranges for so long a period, Guy asked the Mice for some of their pudding. But no sooner had he finished talking than the Mice turned round and sneezed at him! At this scroobious sound Guy rushed back to the boat.

By and by the four children came to a vast, wide plain, on which nothing could be discovered at first. As the travelers walked on there appeared in the distance an object, which seemed to be somebody in a large

white wig, sitting on an armchair made of
sponge cakes and oyster shells. Then the
Quangle Wangle (who had previously been
round the world) exclaimed softly in a loud
voice, "It is the cooperative Cauliflower!"

And it was. They soon found that what
they had taken for the wig was the top of
the Cauliflower, and that he had no feet,
being able to walk on a single stalk—which
saved him the expense of buying shoes.

Presently, while the party from the boat
was gazing at him, he suddenly arose, and,
in a plumdomphious manner, hurried off
toward the setting sun—accompanied by
two Cucumbers—till he finally disappeared
over the brink of the western sky.

Shortly after, the travelers sailed below

some high overhanging rocks, from the top of which a little boy dressed in rose-colored knickerbockers threw an enormous pumpkin at the boat, which hit it and overturned it! Luckily all the party knew how to swim, and they paddled about till after the moon rose, when they righted the boat and boarded it once again.

Two or three days afterward, they came to a place where they found nothing at all except some wide and deep pits full of mulberry jam. This was the property of tiny, yellow-nosed Apes who store up the mulberry jam for their food in winter, when they mix it with pale periwinkle soup, and serve it out in china bowls, which grow freely all over that part of the country. Only

one of the yellow-
nosed Apes was on
the spot and he was
fast asleep, yet the
four travelers, the Quangle
Wangle, and Pussy were so terrified
by the sound of his snoring they merely
took a small cupful of the jam and returned
to their boat without delay.

What was their horror on seeing the boat in the mouth of an enormous Seeze Pyder, a ferocious creature truly dreadful to behold! In a moment, the beautiful boat was bitten into fifty-five thousand million hundred billion bits. It became quite clear that Violet, Slingsby, Guy, and Lionel could no longer carry on their voyage by sea.

The four travelers had to make their way on land. Fortunately, there happened to pass by an elderly Rhinoceros, on which they seized, and, all four mounting on his back—the Quangle Wangle sitting on his horn, and the Pussy Cat swinging at the end of his tail—they set off, having only four small beans and three pounds of mashed potatoes to last them.

They were, however, able to catch numbers of the chickens, turkeys, and other birds who continually landed on the head of the Rhinoceros to gather the seeds of the rhododendron plants which grew there. A crowd of Kangaroos and gigantic Cranes accompanied them, and they went onward in a triumphant procession. In less than eighteen weeks they all arrived safely home, where they were received by their admiring relatives with joy.

How the Cow Jumped Over the Moon

An extract from *The Cat and the Fiddle*
by L. Frank Baum

Little Bobby was the only son of a small farmer who lived out of town upon a country road. Bobby's mother looked after the house and his father took care of the farm. Bobby himself, who was not very big, helped them both as much as he was able.

It was lonely upon the farm, especially when his father and mother were both busy at work, but the boy had one way to amuse

himself that served to pass many an hour
when he would not otherwise have known
what to do. He was very fond of music, and
his father one day brought him from the
town a small fiddle, or violin, which he soon
learned to play upon. I don't suppose he
was a very fine musician, but
the tunes he played pleased
himself, as well as his father
and mother, and Bobby's
fiddle soon became his
constant companion.

   One day in the warm
summer the farmer and his
wife determined to drive to
the town to sell their butter and
eggs and bring back some

groceries in exchange for them. While they were gone Bobby was to be left alone.

"We shall not be back till late in the evening," said his mother, "for the weather is too warm to drive very fast. But I have left you a dish of bread and milk for your supper. Be a good boy and amuse yourself with your fiddle until we return."

Bobby promised to be good and look after the house, and then his father and mother climbed into the wagon and drove away to the town.

The boy was not entirely alone, for there was the big black tabby cat lying upon the floor in the kitchen, and the little yellow dog barking at the wagon as it drove away, and the big moolie cow lowing in the pasture down by the brook. Animals are often very good company, and Bobby did not feel nearly as lonely as he would had there been no living thing about the house.

Besides he had some work to do in the garden, pulling up the weeds that grew thick in the carrot bed. When the last faint sounds of the wheels had died away he went into the garden and began his task.

The little dog went too, for dogs love to be with people and to watch what is going on. He sat down near Bobby and cocked up his ears and wagged his tail, and seemed to take a great interest in Bobby's task of weeding. Once in a while he would rush away to chase a butterfly or bark at a beetle that crawled through the garden, but he always came back to the boy and stayed near his side.

By and by the cat, which found it lonely in the big, empty kitchen, now that Bobby's mother was gone, came walking into the garden also, and lay down upon a path in the sunshine and lazily watched the boy at his work. The dog and the cat were good friends, having lived together so long that they did not care to fight each other. To be sure, Towser (as the little dog was called) sometimes tried to tease pussy, being himself very mischievous. But when the cat put out her sharp claws and showed her teeth, Towser, like a wise little dog, quickly ran away, and so they managed to get along in a friendly manner.

By the time the carrot bed was all weeded, the sun was sinking behind the edge of the forest and the new moon rising in the east. Now Bobby began to feel hungry and went into the house for his dish of bread and milk.

"I think I'll take my supper down to the brook," he said to himself, "and sit upon the grassy bank while I eat it. And I'll take my fiddle, too, and play upon it to pass the time until Father and Mother come home."

It was a good idea, for down by the brook it was cool and pleasant. Bobby took his fiddle under his arm and carried his dish of bread and milk down to the bank that sloped to the edge of the brook. It was rather a steep bank, but Bobby sat upon the edge, and placing his fiddle beside him, leaned against a tree and began to eat his supper.

The little dog had followed at his heels, and the cat also came slowly walking after him. As Bobby ate, they sat one on either side of him and looked earnestly into his face as if they too were hungry. So he threw some of the bread to Towser, who grabbed

it eagerly and swallowed it in the twinkling
of an eye. Bobby left some of the milk in
the dish for the cat, and she came lazily up
and drank it in a dainty, sober fashion, and
licked both the dish and spoon until no drop
of the milk was left.

Then Bobby picked up his fiddle and
tuned it and began to play some of the
pretty tunes he knew. And while he played
he watched the moon rise higher and
higher until it was reflected in the smooth,
still water of the brook. Indeed, Bobby
could not tell which was the plainest to
see, the moon in the sky or the moon in
the water.

The little dog lay quietly on one side of
him, and the cat softly purred upon the

other. Even the moolie cow was attracted by the music and wandered near until she was browsing the grass at the edge of the brook.

After a time, when Bobby had played all the tunes he knew, he laid the fiddle down beside him, near to where the cat slept, and then he lay down upon the bank and began to think.

It is very hard to think long upon a dreamy summer night without falling asleep. Very soon Bobby's eyes closed and he forgot all about the dog and the cat and the cow and the fiddle, and dreamed he was Jack the Giant Killer and was just about to slay the biggest giant in the world.

While he dreamed, the cat sat up and

yawned and stretched herself, and then began wagging her long tail from side to side and watching the moon that was reflected in the water.

But the fiddle lay just behind her, and as she moved her tail, she drew it between the strings of the fiddle, where it caught fast. Then she gave her tail a jerk and pulled the fiddle against the tree, which made a loud noise. This frightened the cat greatly, and not knowing what was the matter with her tail, she started to run as fast as she could. But still the fiddle clung to her tail, and at every step it bounded along and made such a noise that she screamed with terror.

In her fright she ran straight toward the cow, which, seeing a black streak coming at

Nonsense and Gobbledegook

her and hearing the racket made by the fiddle, also became frightened and made such a jump to get out of the way that she leaped right across the brook, over the very spot where the moon shone in the water!

Bobby had been awakened by the noise, and opened his eyes in time to see the cow jump. At first it seemed to him that she had actually jumped over the moon in the sky, instead of the one in the brook.

The little dog laughed to see such fun caused by the cat, and ran barking and dancing along the bank, so that he knocked against the dish, and behold! It slid down the bank, carrying the spoon with it, and the dish ran away with the spoon into the water of the brook with a splash.

As soon as Bobby recovered from his surprise he ran after the cat, which had raced to the house, and soon came to where the fiddle lay upon the ground, it having at last dropped from the cat's tail. He examined it carefully and was glad to find it was not hurt, in spite of its rough usage. Then he had to go across the brook and drive the cow back over the little bridge, and also to roll up his sleeve and reach into the water to recover the dish and the spoon.

Then he went back to the house and lit a lamp, and sat down to while away the time before his father and mother returned by composing a new tune…

Master of All Masters

By Joseph Jacobs

A girl once went to the fair to offer her services as a servant. At last a funny-looking old gentleman hired her and took her home to his house. There, he told her that he had something to teach her, for that in his house he had his own names for many things.

He said to her: "What will you call me?"

"Master or mister, or whatever you

please sir," says she.

He said: "You must call me 'master of all masters.' And what would you call this?" pointing to his bed.

"Bed or couch, or whatever you please, sir."

"No, that's my 'barnacle.' And what do you call these?" said he pointing to his pantaloons.

"Breeches or trousers, or whatever you please, sir."

"You must call them 'squibs and crackers.' And what would you call her?" pointing to the cat.

"Cat or kit, or whatever you please, sir."

"You must call her 'white-faced simminy.' And this now," showing the fire, "what would you call this?"

"Fire or flame, or whatever you please, sir."

"You must call it 'hot cockalorum,' and what would you call this?" he went on, pointing to the water.

"Water or wet, or whatever you please, sir."

"No, 'pondalorum' is its name. And what do you call all this?" asked he, as he pointed to the house.

"House or cottage, or whatever you please, sir."

"You must call it 'high topper mountain,'" said he.

That very night the servant woke her master up in a fright and said:

"Master of all masters, get out of your barnacle and put on your squibs and crackers. For white-faced simminy has got a spark of hot cockalorum on its tail, and unless you get some pondalorum, high topper mountain will be all on hot cockalorum!"

That's all.

The Foolish Weaver

By Andrew Lang

Once there was a weaver who was in want of work, and he took service with a farmer as a shepherd. The farmer knew that the man was very slow-witted and gave him careful instructions as to everything that he was to do. He ended up by saying, "If a wolf or any wild animal tries to hurt the flock, you should pick up a big stone like this"—and he demonstrated—"and throw a few at him. He will be afraid and run away." The weaver said that he understood, and took the sheep off to the hills to graze.

By chance in the afternoon a leopard appeared, so the weaver instantly ran home as fast as he could to get the stones which the farmer had shown him, to throw at the creature. When he came back all the flock were scattered or killed!

When the farmer found out he gave the weaver a sound scolding. "Were there no stones on the hillside?" he cried. "You didn't have to run

52

back here and get these exact ones! You are not fit to herd sheep. Today you shall stay at home and mind my sick mother—perhaps you will be able to drive flies off her face, if you can't drive beasts away from sheep!"

So, the weaver was left at home to take care of the farmer's old, sick mother. Now as she lay outside on a bed, it turned out that the flies became very troublesome. The weaver looked round for something to drive them away with, and as he had been told to pick up the nearest stone to drive the beasts away from the flock, he thought he would this time show how cleverly he could obey orders. He seized the nearest stone, which was a big, heavy one, and tossed it at the flies. Of course, very unhappily, he killed the

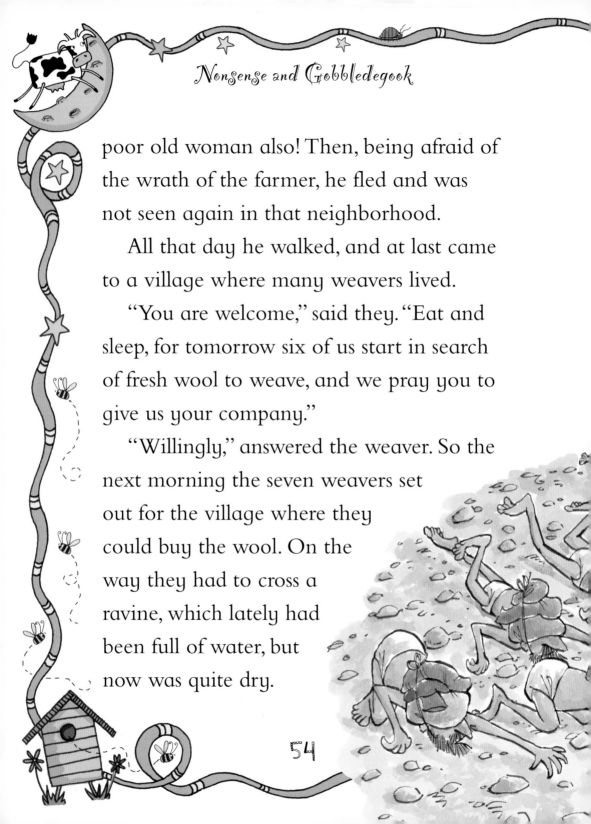

poor old woman also! Then, being afraid of the wrath of the farmer, he fled and was not seen again in that neighborhood.

All that day he walked, and at last came to a village where many weavers lived.

"You are welcome," said they. "Eat and sleep, for tomorrow six of us start in search of fresh wool to weave, and we pray you to give us your company."

"Willingly," answered the weaver. So the next morning the seven weavers set out for the village where they could buy the wool. On the way they had to cross a ravine, which lately had been full of water, but now was quite dry.

The Foolish Weaver

However, the weavers were accustomed to swimming over this ravine. Regardless of the fact that it was dry, they stripped and, tying their clothes on their heads, started to swim across the dry sand and rocks that formed the bed of the ravine.

The weavers all got to the other side with bruised knees and elbows, and one of them began to count everybody to make sure that all were there. He counted all except himself, and then cried out that somebody was missing! This set each of them counting, but each made the same mistake of counting all except himself, so that they became certain that one of them was missing! They ran up and down the bank of the ravine in distress, looking for signs of their lost comrade.

Then a farmer found them and asked what was the matter. "Alas!" said one. "Seven of us started from the other bank and one must have been drowned on the crossing, as we can only find six remaining!"

Picking up his stick, the farmer dealt each a sounding blow, counting as he did so, "One! Two! Three!" and so on up to seven.

When the weavers found that there were seven of them they were full of gratitude for the man whom they thought must be a magician—for he could make seven out of what was obviously just six people.

Boots Who Made the Princess Say, "That's a Story"

By Sir George Webbe Dasent

Once upon a time there was a king who had a daughter, and she was such a dreadful storyteller that the like of her was not to be found far or near. So the king sent out word that if anyone could tell such a string of lies that would get her to say, "That's a story," he could have her for his wife, and half the kingdom too. Many came to try their luck, for everyone would have been very glad to have the Princess, to say nothing of the kingdom. But they all cut a sorry figure, for the Princess was so given to storytelling that their lies went in one ear and out the other.

Among the rest came three brothers. The two elder went first, but they fared no better than those who had gone before. Last of all, the third brother, Boots, set off and found the Princess in the farmyard.

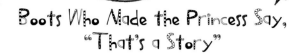

Boots Who Made the Princess Say,
"That's a Story"

"Good morning," he said, "and thank you for nothing."

"Good morning," said she, "and the same to you."

Then she went on, "You haven't such a fine farmyard as ours, I'll be bound. For when two shepherds stand, one at each end of it, and blow their ram's horns, one can't hear the other."

"Haven't we though!" answered Boots. "Ours is far bigger. For when a cow begins to go with calf at one end of it, she doesn't get to the other end before the time to drop her calf is come."

"I dare say!" said the Princess. "Well, but you haven't such a big ox, after all, as ours yonder. For when two men sit, one on each horn, they can't touch each other with a ginormous ruler."

"Stuff!" said Boots. "Is that all? Why, we have an ox who is so big, that when two men sit, one on each horn, and each blows his great mountain trumpet, they can't hear one another."

"I dare say," said the Princess. "But you haven't so much milk as we, I'll be bound.

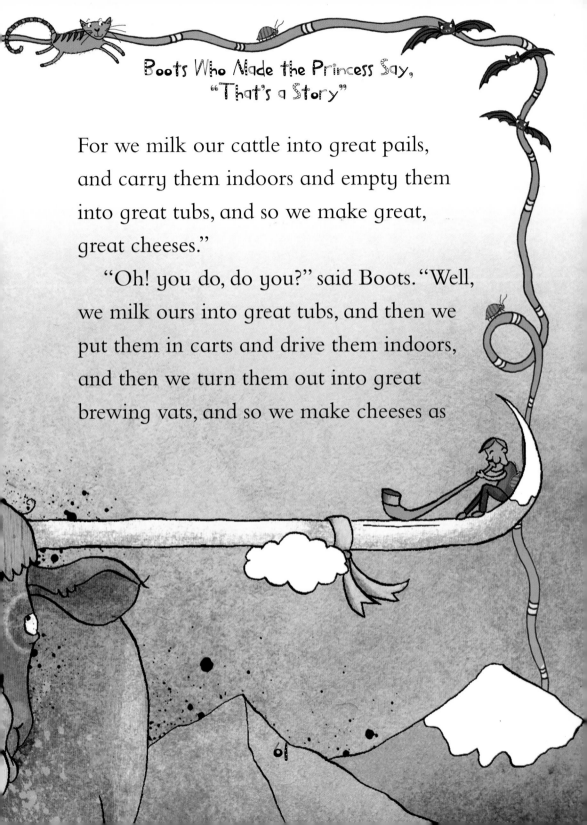

For we milk our cattle into great pails,
and carry them indoors and empty them
into great tubs, and so we make great,
great cheeses."

"Oh! you do, do you?" said Boots. "Well,
we milk ours into great tubs, and then we
put them in carts and drive them indoors,
and then we turn them out into great
brewing vats, and so we make cheeses as

61

big as a great house. We had, too, a pony to
tread the cheese well together when it was
making, but once she tumbled down into
the cheese, and we lost her. After we had
eaten at this cheese seven years, we came
upon the pony, alive and kicking.

"Well, once after that I was going to
drive this pony to the mill, and her
backbone snapped in two, but I wasn't put
out, not I, for I took a young tree, and put it
into her for a backbone, and she had no
other backbone all the while we had her.
But the sapling grew up into such a tall
tree, that I climbed right up to heaven by it,
and when I got there, I saw the Virgin Mary
sitting and spinning the foam of the sea into
pigs'-bristle ropes. But just then the tree

broke short off, and I couldn't get down again, so the Virgin Mary let me down by one of the ropes. Down I slipped, straight into a fox's hole, and who should sit there but my mother and your father cobbling shoes. Just as I stepped in, my mother gave your father such a box on the ear, that it made his whiskers curl."

"That's a story!" said the Princess. "My father never did any such thing in all his born days!"

So Boots got to marry the Princess and won half the kingdom besides.

A Silly Question

By E. Nesbit

"**H**ow do you come to be white, when all your brothers are tabby?" Dolly asked her kitten. As she spoke, she took it away from the ball it was playing with, and held it up and looked in its face as Alice did with the Red Queen.

"I'll tell you if you'll keep it a secret, and not hold me so tight," the kitten answered.

Dolly was not surprised to hear the

kitten speak, for she had read fairy books and she knew that all creatures answer if one only speaks to them properly. So she held the kitten more comfortably and the tale began.

"You must know, my dear Dolly," the kitten began, sounding as though it had always known Dolly very well, "you must know that when we were very small we all set out to seek our fortunes—"

"Why," interrupted Dolly, "you were all born and brought up in our barn! I used to see you every day."

"Quite so," said the kitten, "we sought our fortune every night, and it turned out to be mice, mostly. Well, one night I was seeking mine, when I came to a hole in the door that I had never noticed before. I crept through it and found myself in a beautiful large room. It smelled delicious. There was cheese there, and fish, and cream, and mice, and milk. It was the most lovely room you can think of."

"There's no such room—" began Dolly.

"Well, I stayed there some time," continued the kitten. "It was the happiest hour of my life. But, as I was washing my face after one of the most delicious herring's heads you ever tasted, I noticed that on nails all round the room were hung skins— and they were cat skins," the kitten added slowly. "Well may you tremble!"

Dolly hadn't trembled. She had only shaken the kitten to make it speak faster.

"Well, I stood there rooted to the ground with horror, and then came a sort of horrible scramble-rush, and a barking and squeaking, and a terrible monster stood before me. It was something like a dog and something like a broom, something like being thrown out of the larder by cook—I can't describe it. It caught me up, and in less than a moment it had hung my tabby skin on a nail behind the door. I crept out of that lovely fairyland a cat without a skin. And that's how I came to be white."

"I don't quite see—" began Dolly.

"No? Why, what would your mother do if someone took off your dress, and hung it on a nail where she could not get it?"

"Buy me another, I suppose."

"Exactly. But when my mother took me to the cat-skin shop, they were, unfortunately, quite out of tabby dresses in my size, so I had to have a white one."

"I don't believe a word of it," said Dolly.

"No? Well, I'm sure it's as good a story as you could expect in answer to such a silly question."

"But you were always—"

"Oh, well!" said the kitten, showing its claws, "if you know more about it than I do, of course there's no more to be said. Perhaps you could tell me why your hair is brown?"

"I was born so, I believe," said Dolly gently.

The kitten put its nose in the air.

"You've got no imagination," it said.

"But Kitty, really and truly, without pretending, you were born white, you know."

"If you know all about it, why did you ask me? At any rate, you can't expect me to remember whether I was born white or not. I was too young to notice such things."

"Now you are in fun," said poor Dolly, bewildered.

The kitten bristled with indignation.

"What! You really don't believe me? I'll never speak to you again," the kitten said. And it never has.

The History of the Seven Families of the Lake Pipple-Popple

By Edward Lear

Introductory

In former days—that is to say, once upon a time—there lived in the Land of Gramble-Blamble seven families. They lived by the side of the great Lake Pipple-Popple (one of the seven families, indeed, lived in the lake), and on the outskirts of the city of Tosh. The names of all these places you have probably heard of and you have only not to look in your geography books to find out about them.

Now, the seven families who lived on the borders of the great Lake Pipple-Popple were as follows in the next chapter.

The Seven Families

There was a family of two old Parrots and seven young Parrots.

There was a family of two old Storks and seven young Storks.

There was a family of two old Geese and seven young Geese.

There was a family of two old Owls and seven young Owls.

72

There was a family of two old Guinea Pigs and seven young Guinea Pigs.

There was a family of two old Cats and seven young Cats.

And there was a family of two old Fishes and seven young Fishes.

The Habits of the Seven Families

The Parrots lived upon the beautiful Soffsky-Poffsky trees, which were covered with blue leaves, and they fed upon fruit, artichokes, and striped beetles.

The Storks walked in and out of the Lake Pipple-Popple, and ate frogs for breakfast, and buttered toast for tea, but on account of the extreme length of their legs they could not sit down, and so they walked about continually.

The Geese, having webs to their feet, caught quantities of flies, which they ate for dinner.

The Owls anxiously looked after mice, which they caught, and made into sago puddings.

The Guinea Pigs toddled about the gardens, and ate lettuces and Cheshire cheese.

The Cats sat still in the sunshine, and fed upon sponge biscuits.

The Fishes lived in the lake, and fed chiefly on boiled periwinkles.

And all these seven families lived together in the utmost fun and happiness.

The Children of the Seven Families Are Sent Away

One day all the seven fathers and the seven mothers of the seven families agreed to send their children out to see the world.

They called them all together, and gave them each eight shillings and some good advice, some chocolate drops, and a small green Morocco pocket book to write down what they had spent in, and begged them above all *not to quarrel.* Then the children of each family thanked their parents, and,

75

making in all forty-nine polite bows, they
went into the wide world.

The History of the Seven Young Parrots

The seven young Parrots had not gone far
when they saw a tree with a single cherry
on it, which the oldest Parrot picked
instantly, but the other six, being extremely
hungry, tried to get it also. On which all the
seven began to fight, and they scuffled, and
huffled, and ruffled, and shuffled, and
puffled, and muffled, and buffled, and
duffled, and fluffled, and guffled, and
bruffled, and screamed, and shrieked, and
squealed, and squeaked, and clawed, and
snapped, and bit, and bumped, and

thumped, and dumped, and flumped each other, till they were all torn into little bits. At last there was nothing left to record this painful incident except the cherry and seven small green feathers.

And that was the end of the seven young Parrots.

The History of the Seven Young Storks

When the seven young Storks set out, they walked or flew for fourteen weeks in a straight line, and for six weeks more in a crooked one, and then they ran as hard as they could for one hundred and eight miles. After that they stood still and made a chatter-clatter-blattery noise with their bills.

About the same time they saw a large frog, spotted with green, and with a sky-blue stripe under each ear. So, being hungry, they immediately flew at him, and began to quarrel as to which of his legs should be taken off first. One said this and another said that, and while they were all quarreling, the frog hopped away.

When they saw that he was gone, they began to chatter-clatter, blatter-platter, patter-blatter, matter-

clatter, flatter-quatter, more violently than
ever. After they had fought for a week, they
pecked each other all to little pieces, so that
at last nothing was left of any of them
except their bills.

And that was the end of the seven
young Storks.

The History of the Seven Young Geese

When the seven young Geese began
to travel, they went over a large
plain, on which there was but one
tree. So four of them went up to the
top of it and looked about them,
while the other three waddled up and
down and repeated poetry.

79

Presently they saw, a long way off, a curious object with a perfectly round body resembling a boiled plum pudding, with two little wings, and a beak, and three feathers growing out of his head, and only one leg.

So, after a time, all the seven young Geese said to each other, "Beyond all doubt this beast must be a Plum-pudding Flea!"

The Plum-pudding Flea began to hop and skip on his one leg and came straight to the tree, where he stopped and looked about him angrily.

The seven young Geese were greatly alarmed, and all of a tremble-bemble.

The Plum-pudding Flea skipped and hopped about more and more, and higher and higher. Then he opened his mouth and

began to bark so loudly
that they were
unable to bear the
noise and every one
of them suddenly
tumbled down
quite dead.

So that was the end of the
seven young Geese.

The History of the Seven Young Owls

When the seven young Owls set out, they
sat every now and then on the branches of
old trees, and never went far at one time.
One night, when it was quite dark, they
thought they heard a mouse, but, as the gas

lamps were not lit, they could not see him.

So they called out, "Is that a mouse?"

On which a mouse answered, "Squeaky-peeky-weeky! Yes, it is!"

Immediately all the young Owls threw themselves off the tree, meaning to land on the ground, but they did not see that there was a large well below them, into which they all fell, and every one of them was drowned in less than half a minute.

And that was the end of the seven young Owls.

The History of the Seven Young Guinea Pigs

The seven young Guinea Pigs went into a garden full of gooseberry bushes and tiggory trees, under which they fell asleep. When they awoke, they saw a large lettuce, which had grown out of the ground while they had been sleeping, and which had an immense number of delicious-looking green leaves. Instantly the seven young Guinea Pigs rushed with such extreme force against the lettuce plant, and hit their heads so hard against its stalk, that all seven were killed.

That was the end of the seven young Guinea Pigs.

The History of the Seven Young Cats

The seven young Cats set off on their travels with great delight. But, on coming to the top of a high hill, they perceived a

Clangle Wangle and ran straight up to it.

Now, the Clangle Wangle is a most dangerous beast, and by no means commonly to be met with. The moment the Clangle Wangle saw the seven young Cats approach, he ran away. As he ran straight on for four months, and the Cats, though they continued to run, could never overtake him, they all gradually died of exhaustion, and never afterward recovered.

And that was the end of the seven young Cats.

The History of the Seven Young Fishes

The seven young Fishes swam across the Lake Pipple-Popple, and into the river, and into the ocean, where, most unhappily for them, they saw, on the fifteenth day of their travels, a bright-blue Boss-Woss, and instantly swam after him. But the Blue Boss-Woss plunged into soft mud where, in fact, his house was. And the seven young Fishes also plunged into the mud quite against their will, and, not being accustomed to it, were all suffocated in a very short period.

And that was the end of the seven young Fishes.

Of What Occurred Subsequently

After it was known that the seven young Parrots, and the seven young Storks, and the seven young Geese, and the seven young

Owls, and the seven young Guinea Pigs, and the seven young Cats, and the seven young Fishes, were all dead, the Frog, and the Plum-pudding Flea, and the Mouse, and the Clangle Wangle, and the Blue Boss-Woss, all met together to rejoice. They gave a tea party, and a garden party, and a ball, and a concert, and then returned to their respective homes full of joy.

Of What Became of the Parents of the Forty-Nine Children

When the two old Parrots, and the two old Storks, and the two old Geese, and the two old Owls, and the two old Guinea Pigs, and the two old Cats, and the two old Fishes, became aware, by reading in the newspapers, of the tragic death of the whole of their families, they refused all further food. Sending out to various shops, they purchased great quantities of Cayenne pepper and brandy and vinegar and blue sealing wax, besides seven immense glass bottles with airtight stoppers. And, having done this, they ate a light supper of brown bread and Jerusalem artichokes, and said goodbye to all their friends.

Conclusion

After this they filled the bottles with the ingredients for pickling, and each couple jumped into a separate bottle, by which effort, of course, they all died immediately, and became thoroughly pickled in a few minutes. They had left strict orders that the stoppers of the seven bottles should be carefully sealed up with the blue sealing wax they had purchased, and that they themselves, in the bottles, should be presented to the principal museum of the city of Tosh, and to be placed on a marble table with silver-gilt legs, for admiration every day by the public.

And if you ever happen to go to Gramble-Blamble, and visit that museum in the city of Tosh, look for them on the ninety-eighth table in the four hundred and twenty-seventh room of the right-hand corridor of the left wing of the central quadrangle of that magnificent building. For, if you do not, you certainly will not see them.

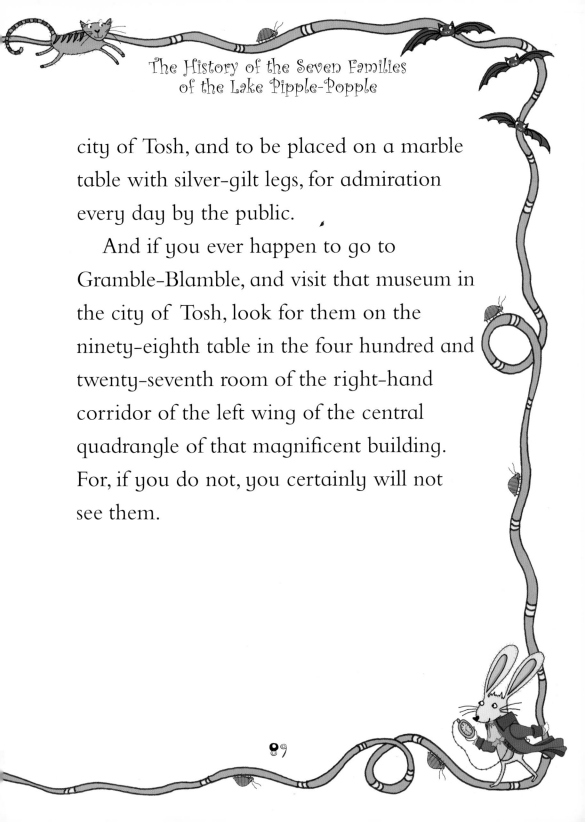

The Finest Liar in the World

By Andrew Lang

At the edge of a wood there lived an old man who had only one son. One day he called the boy to him and said he wanted some grain ground, but the youth must be sure never to enter any mill where the miller was beardless.

The boy took the grain and set out.

Before he had gone very far he saw a large mill in front of him, with a beardless man standing in the doorway.

"Good greeting, beardless one!" cried he.

"Good greeting, sonny," replied the man.

"Could I grind something here?"

"Yes, certainly! I will finish what I am doing and then you can grind as long as you like."

But suddenly the boy remembered what his father had told him, and bade farewell to the man. He went further down the river till he came to another mill, not knowing that as soon as his back was turned the beardless man had picked up a bag of grain and run hastily to the same mill before him.

When the boy reached the second mill, and saw a second beardless man sitting there, he did not stop, and walked on till he came to a third mill. But this time also the beardless man had been too clever for him, and had arrived first by another road. When it happened a fourth time the boy grew cross. He said to himself, "It is no good going on. There seems to be a beardless man in every mill," and he took his sack from his back, and made up his mind to grind his grain where he was.

The beardless man finished grinding his

own grain, and when he had done he said to the boy, who was beginning to grind his, "Suppose, sonny, we make a cake of what you have there."

Now the boy had been rather uneasy when he remembered his father's words, but he thought to himself, 'What is done cannot be undone,' and answered, "Very well, let it be."

Then the beardless one got up, threw the flour into the tub and made a hole in the middle, telling the boy to fetch some water from the river in his two hands to mix the cake. When the cake was ready for baking they put it on the fire, and covered it with hot ashes, till it was cooked through. Then they leaned it up against the wall, for it was too big to go into a cupboard, and the beardless one said to the boy: "Look here, sonny, if we share this cake we shall neither of us have enough. Let us see who can tell the biggest lie, and the one who lies the best shall have the whole cake."

The boy, not knowing what else to do, answered, "All right, you begin."

So the beardless one began to lie with all his might, and when he was tired of inventing new lies the boy said to him, "My good fellow, if *that* is all you can do it is not much! Listen to me, and I will tell you a true story.

"In my youth, when I was an old man, we had a quantity of beehives. Every morning when I got up I counted them over, and it was quite easy to number the bees, but I never could reckon the hives properly. One day, as I was counting the bees, I discovered that my best bee was missing, and without losing a moment I saddled a cock and went out to look for him. I traced him as far as the shore, and knew that he had crossed the sea, and that I must follow. When I had reached the other side I found a man had harnessed my bee to a plow, and with his help was sowing millet seed.

"I shouted to him, 'That is my bee! Where did you get him from?'

"The man replied, 'Brother, if he is yours, take him,' and he not only gave me back my bee, but a sack of millet seed into the

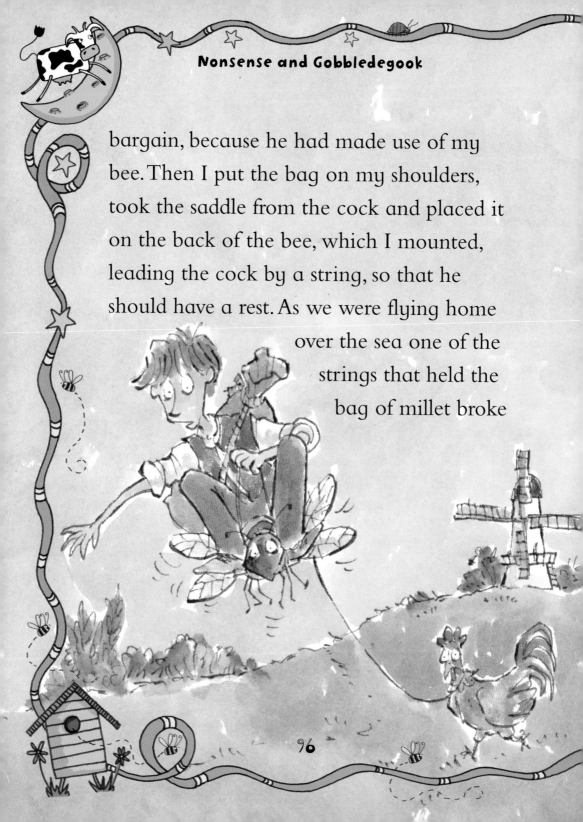

bargain, because he had made use of my bee. Then I put the bag on my shoulders, took the saddle from the cock and placed it on the back of the bee, which I mounted, leading the cock by a string, so that he should have a rest. As we were flying home over the sea one of the strings that held the bag of millet broke in two, and the sack dropped straight into the ocean. It was quite lost, of course, and there was no use thinking about it, and by the time we were safe back again night had come. I then got down from my bee, and let him loose so that he might get his supper, gave the cock some hay, and went to sleep myself. But when I awoke with the sun what a scene met my eyes! During the night, wolves had come and had eaten my bee. And honey lay ankle-deep in the valley and knee-deep on the hills. Then I began to consider how I could best collect some to take home with me.

"Now it happened that I had with me a small hatchet, and this I took to the wood, hoping to meet some animal which I could kill, whose skin I might turn into a bag. As I entered the forest I saw two roe deer hopping on one foot, so I slew them with a single blow, and made three bags from their skins, all of which I filled with honey and placed on the back of the cock.

"At length I reached home, where I was told that my father had just been born, and that I must go to fetch some holy water to sprinkle him with. As I went I turned over in my mind if there was no way for me to get back my millet seed, which had dropped into the sea. When I arrived at the place with the holy water I saw the seed had fallen on fruitful soil, and was growing before my eyes. More than that, it was cut by an invisible hand and made into a cake.

"So I took the cake as well as the holy water, and was flying back with them over the sea, when there fell a great rain, and the sea was swollen, and swept away my millet cake. Ah, how vexed I was at its loss when I was safe on earth again.

"Suddenly I remembered that my hair was very long. If I stood it touched the ground, although if I was sitting it only reached my ears. I seized a knife and cut off a large lock, which I plaited together, and, when night came, tied it into a knot and prepared to use it for a pillow. But what was I to do for a fire? A tinder box I had, but no wood. Then it occurred to me that I had stuck a needle in my clothes, so I took the needle and split it in pieces, and lit it, then

laid myself down by the fire and went to
sleep. But while I was sleeping a spark from
the fire lighted on the hair, which was
burned up in a moment. In despair I threw
myself on the ground, and
instantly sank in it as
far as my waist. I
struggled to get
out but only fell
in further, so I ran to
the house, seized a spade, dug myself out,
and took home the holy water.

"On the way I noticed that the ripe
fields were full of reapers, and suddenly the
air became so frightfully hot that the men
dropped down in a faint. Then I called to
them, 'Why don't you bring out our mare,

which is as tall as two days and as broad as half a day, and make a shade for yourselves?' My father heard what I said and jumped quickly on the mare, and the reapers worked with a will in the shadow, while I snatched up a wooden pail to bring them some water to drink.

"When I got to the well it was frozen hard. In order to draw some water I had to take off my head and break the ice with it. As I drew near them, carrying the water, the reapers all cried out, 'What has become of your head?' I put up my hand and discovered that I really had no head, and that I must have left it in the well. I ran back for it, but found that a fox which was passing by had pulled my head out of the

water and was tearing at it. I crept up to
him, and gave him such a kick that he
uttered a loud scream, and let fall a
parchment on which was written:
THE CAKE IS MINE AND THE BEARDLESS
ONE GOES EMPTY-HANDED."

With these words the boy rose, took the
cake, and went home, while the beardless
one was left to swallow
his disappointment.

A Most Curious Country

An extract from *Through the Looking Glass*
by Lewis Carroll

*At home one day, Alice falls through a looking glass
into the strange world beyond, where weirder and weirder
things happen to her…*

For some minutes Alice stood without
speaking, looking out in all directions over
the country—and a most curious country it
was. There were a number of tiny little
brooks running straight across it from side
to side, and the ground between was divided
up into squares by a number of little green

hedges, that reached from brook to brook.

"I declare it's marked out just like a large chessboard!" Alice said at last. "There ought to be some men moving about somewhere —and so there are!" she added in a tone of delight, and her heart began to beat quick with excitement as she went on. "It's a great huge game of chess that's being played —all over the world—if this *is* the world at all, you know. Oh, what fun it is! How I *wish* I was one of them! I wouldn't mind being a Pawn, if only I might join—though of course I should *like* to be a Queen best."

She glanced rather shyly at the real Queen as she said this, who smiled pleasantly, and said, "That's easily managed. You can

be the White Queen's Pawn, if you like, as
you're in the Second Square to begin with.
When you get to the Eighth Square you'll
be a Queen…" Just at this moment,
somehow or other, they began to run.

Alice never could quite make out, in
thinking it over afterward, how it was that
they began. All she remembers is, that they
were running hand in hand, and the Queen
went so fast that it was all she could do to
keep up with her, and still the Queen kept
crying, "Faster! Faster!" but Alice felt she
could not go faster, though she had no breath
left to say so.

The most curious part of the thing was,
that the trees and the other things round
them never changed their places at all:

however fast they went, they never seemed to pass anything. 'I wonder if all the things move along with us?' thought poor puzzled Alice. And the Queen seemed to guess her thoughts, for she cried, "Faster! Don't try to talk!"

Not that Alice had any idea of doing *that*. She felt as if she would never be able to talk again, she was getting so much out of breath, and still the Queen cried "Faster! Faster!" and dragged her along.

"Are we nearly there?" Alice managed to pant out at last.

"Nearly there!" the Queen repeated. "Why, we passed it ten minutes ago! Faster!" And they ran on for a time in silence, with the wind whistling in Alice's ears, and almost blowing her hair off her head, she fancied.

"Now! Now!" cried the Queen. "Faster! Faster!" And they went so fast that at last they seemed to skim through the air, hardly touching the ground with their feet, till suddenly, just as Alice was getting quite exhausted, they stopped, and she found herself sitting on the ground, breathless and giddy.

The Queen propped her up against a tree, and said, "You may rest a little now."

Alice looked round her in great surprise. "I do believe we've been under this tree the whole time! Everything's just as it was!"

"Of course it is," said the Queen, "what would you have it?"

"Well, in *our* country," said Alice, still panting a little, "you'd generally get to somewhere else—if you ran very fast for a long time, as we've been doing."

"A slow sort of country!" said the Queen. "Now, *here*, you see, it takes all the running *you* can do, to keep in the same place. If you want to get somewhere else, you must run at least twice as fast as that!"

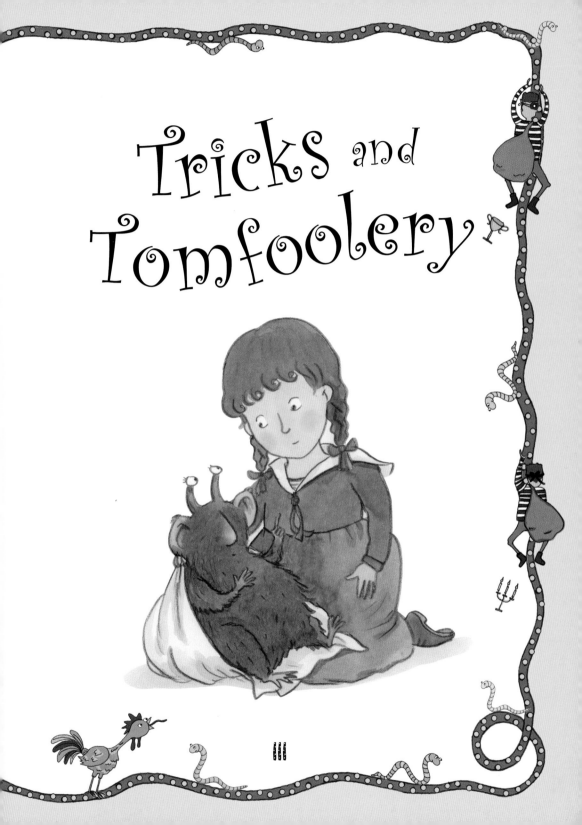

Tricks and Tomfoolery

111

The Traveling Musicians

By the Brothers Grimm

An honest farmer once had a donkey that had been a faithful servant to him for a great many years. But it was now growing old and every day more and more unfit for work. His master therefore was tired of keeping him and began to think of getting rid of him. The donkey, who saw that some mischief was in the wind, took himself slyly off, and began his journey toward the great city. 'For there,' he thought, 'I may become a musician and make my fortune that way.'

After he had traveled a little way, he spied a dog lying by the roadside and panting as if he were tired. "What makes you pant so, my friend?" said the donkey.

"Alas," said the dog, "my master was going to knock me on the head because I am old and weak and can no longer make myself useful to him in hunting, so I ran away. What can I do to earn my living?"

"Listen to this," said the donkey, "I am going to the great city to become a musician. Suppose you come with me, and try what you can do in the same way?"

The dog said he was willing, and they jogged on together.

They had not gone far before they saw a cat sitting in the middle of the road, looking most downcast. "Hello there, my good lady," said the donkey, "what's the matter with you? You look quite out of spirits!"

"Ah, me!" said the cat. "How can one be in good spirits when one's life is in danger? Because I am beginning to grow old, and had rather lie at my ease by the fire than run about the house after mice, my mistress caught me by the scruff of the neck and was going to drown me. Though I have been lucky enough to get away from her, I do not know what is to become of me."

"Oh," said the donkey, "by all means

come with us to the great city. You are a good night singer and may make your fortune as a musician."

The cat was pleased with the thought, and joined the party.

Soon afterward, as they were passing by a farmyard, they saw a rooster perched upon a gate, and screaming out with all his might and main.

"Bravo!" said the donkey. "Upon my word, you make a famous noise. Pray, what is all this about?"

"Why," said the rooster, "I was just now saying that we should have fine weather for our washing day. Yet my mistress and the cook don't thank me for my pains, but threaten to cut off my head tomorrow, and make broth of me for the guests that are coming on Sunday!"

"Heaven forbid!" said the donkey. "Come with us, Master Rooster. It will be better, at any rate, than staying here to have your head cut off! Besides, who knows? If we care to sing in tune, we may get up some kind of a concert, so come along with us."

"With all my heart," said the rooster, so they all four went on happily together.

They could not, however, reach the great city the first day. So when night came on, they went into a wood to sleep. The donkey and the dog laid themselves down under a great tree, and the cat climbed up into the branches. The rooster, thinking that the

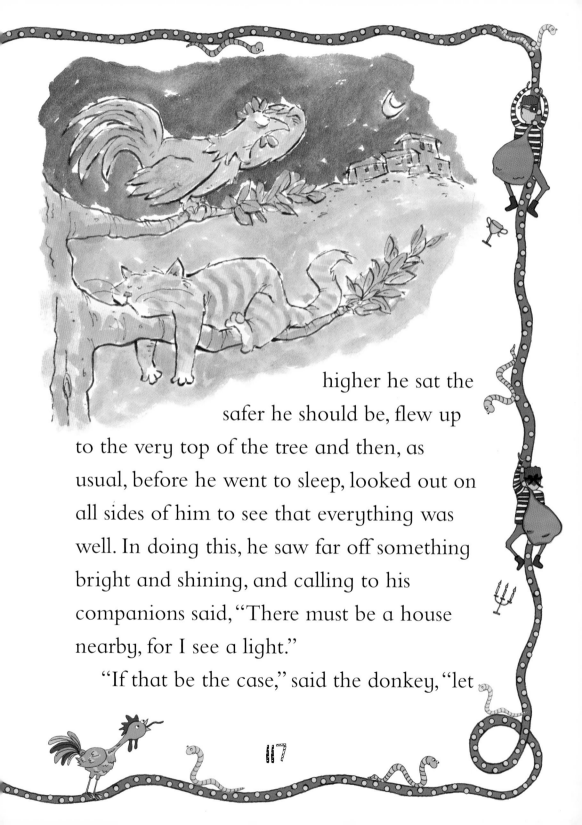

higher he sat the
safer he should be, flew up
to the very top of the tree and then, as
usual, before he went to sleep, looked out on
all sides of him to see that everything was
well. In doing this, he saw far off something
bright and shining, and calling to his
companions said, "There must be a house
nearby, for I see a light."

"If that be the case," said the donkey, "let

us go and see if we can stay there, for our current arrangement is hardly the best in the world!"

"Besides," added the dog, "I should not be the worse for a bone or two, or a nice bit of meat."

So they walked off together toward the spot where the rooster had seen the light. As they drew near the light, it became larger and brighter, till they at last came close to a house.

Little did the unfortunate band of animals know that it was a house in which a gang of robbers lived.

The donkey, being the tallest of the company, marched up to the window and peeped in. "Well, Donkey," said the rooster, "what do you see?"

"What do I see?" replied the donkey. "Why, I see a table spread with all kinds of good things, and robbers sitting round it making merry."

"That would be a perfect lodging place for us," said the rooster.

"Yes," said the donkey, "if we could only get in." So they put their heads together and thought hard about how they might be able to get the robbers out, and at last they hit upon a plan.

The donkey placed himself upright on his hind legs, with his forefeet resting against the window. The dog got upon his back, the cat scrambled up to the dog's shoulders, and the rooster flew up and sat

upon the cat's head. When all was ready a
signal was given, and they began their
music. The donkey brayed, the dog barked,
the cat mewed, and the rooster screamed.
Then they all broke through the window at
once, and came tumbling into the room,
among the broken glass, with a most
hideous clatter!

The robbers, who had been not a little
frightened by the opening concert, had now
no doubt that some frightful hobgoblin had
broken in upon them, and scampered away
as fast as they could.

Once the coast was clear, our travelers
sat down and gobbled up what the robbers
had left with eagerness. As soon as they had
satisfied themselves, they put out the lights,

and each once more sought out a
resting place to his own liking. The
donkey laid himself down upon a
heap of straw in the yard, the dog stretched
himself upon a mat behind the door, the cat
curled up on the hearth before the warm
ashes, and the rooster perched upon a beam
on the top of the house. They were all tired
with their journey, and soon fell asleep.

About midnight, when the robbers saw
from afar that the lights were out and all
seemed quiet, they began to think that they
had been in too great a hurry to run away.
One of them went to see what was going
on. Finding everything still, he marched into
the kitchen and groped about till he found
a match to light a candle. Then, spying the

glittering fiery eyes of the cat, he mistook them for live coals, and held the match to them to light it. The cat, not understanding this joke, sprang at his face and scratched at him. This frightened the robber dreadfully, and away he ran to the back door. There the dog jumped up and bit him on the leg, and as he was crossing over the yard the donkey kicked him, and the rooster, who had been awakened by the noise, crowed with all his might.

At this the robber ran back as fast as he could to his comrades, and told the captain how a horrid witch had got into the house, and had spat at him and scratched his face with her long bony fingers, how a man with a knife in his hand had hidden himself behind the door and stabbed him in the leg, how a black monster stood in the yard and struck him with a club, and how the devil had sat upon the top of the house and cried, "Throw the rascal up here!"

After this the robbers never dared to go back to the house. The musicians were so pleased with their quarters that they took up their abode there, and there they are, I dare say, to this very day.

The Field of Boliauns

By Joseph Jacobs

One fine day at harvest, in holiday time, when the sun blazed high over the grainfields, Tom Fitzpatrick was taking a ramble through the country. He went along the shady side of a field, when all of a sudden he heard a clacking sort of noise a little before him in the hedgerow.

"Dear me," said Tom, "but isn't it surprising to hear the stone-chatters singing so late in the season?" So Tom stole on, going on the tips of his toes to try to get a sight of what was making the noise, to see if he was right in his guess.

The noise stopped, but as Tom looked sharply through the bushes, what should he see in a nook of the hedge but a brown jug, that might hold about a gallon and a half of liquid. By and by a little wee teeny-tiny bit of an old man sauntered up, with a jaunty little hat stuck upon the top of his head. He pulled out a little wooden stool and

stood up upon it, then dipped a little mug
into the pitcher, took it out full and put it
beside the stool. Then he sat down under
the pitcher, and began to work at cobbling
a shoe, putting a heel piece on a pointy-
toed shoe just fit for himself.

"Well, by the powers," said Tom to
himself, "I often heard tell of the
Leprechauns, and, to tell God's truth, I
never rightly believed in them—but
here's one of them in real earnest. If I
play my cards right, I can
make my fortune. They say a
body must never take their eyes
off them, or they'll escape."

Tom now stole on a little
further, with his eye fixed on the

little man just as a cat does with a mouse. When he got up quite close to him, "God bless your work, neighbor," said Tom.

The little man raised up his head, and, "Thank you kindly," said he.

"I wonder why you'd be working on the holiday!" said Tom.

"That's my own business, not yours," was the reply.

"Well, maybe you'd be civil enough to tell us what you've got in the jug there?" said Tom.

"That I will, with pleasure," said he. "It's good beer."

"Beer!" said Tom. "Thunder and fire! Where did you get it?"

"Where did I get it, is it? Why, I made it.

And what do you think I made it of?"

"I haven't a clue," said Tom. "Malt, I suppose, at a guess."

"Wrong!" announced the brownie gleefully. "I made it of heath."

"Of heath!" said Tom, bursting out laughing. "Sure you don't think me to be such a fool as to believe that?"

"Do as you please," said he, "but what I tell you is the truth. Did you never hear tell of the Vikings?"

"Well, what about them?" said Tom.

"Why, when they were here they taught us to make beer out of the heath, and the secret's been in my family ever since."

"Will you give me a taste of your beer?" said Tom.

"I'll tell you what it is, young man, it would be fitter for you to be looking after your father's property than to be bothering decent quiet people with your foolish questions. There now, while you're idling away your time here, the cows have broken into the oats, and are knocking the corn all about."

Tom was taken so by surprise with this that he was just on the very point of turning round… but he suddenly realized that the Leprechaun might be up to a trick. He collected himself, made a grab at the Leprechaun, and caught him up in his hand. However, in his hurry he knocked over the jug and spilled all the beer, so that he could not get a taste of it to tell what sort it was.

Tom then swore that he would kill the Leprechaun if he did not show him where his money was.

Tom looked so wicked and determined that the little man was quite frightened, so said the Leprechaun, "Come along with me a couple of fields off and I will show you a crock of gold."

So they went, and Tom held the Leprechaun fast in his hand, and never took his eyes off him. They had to cross hedges and ditches, and a crooked bit of bog, till at last they came to a great field all full of boliaun plants. The Leprechaun pointed to a big boliaun, and says he, "Dig under that boliaun, and you'll get the great crock all full of guineas."

Tom, in his hurry, had never thought of bringing a spade with him, so he made up his mind to run home and fetch one. So that he might find the right spot when he returned, he took off the red garter on his arm and tied it round the boliaun plant.

Then Tom said to the Leprechaun, "Swear that you won't take that garter away from that boliaun." And the Leprechaun swore not to touch it.

"I suppose," said the Leprechaun, very civilly, "you have no further need of me?"

"No," says Tom, "you may go away now, if you please, and God speed you, and may good luck attend you wherever you go."

"Well, goodbye to you, Tom Fitzpatrick," said the Leprechaun, "and much good may

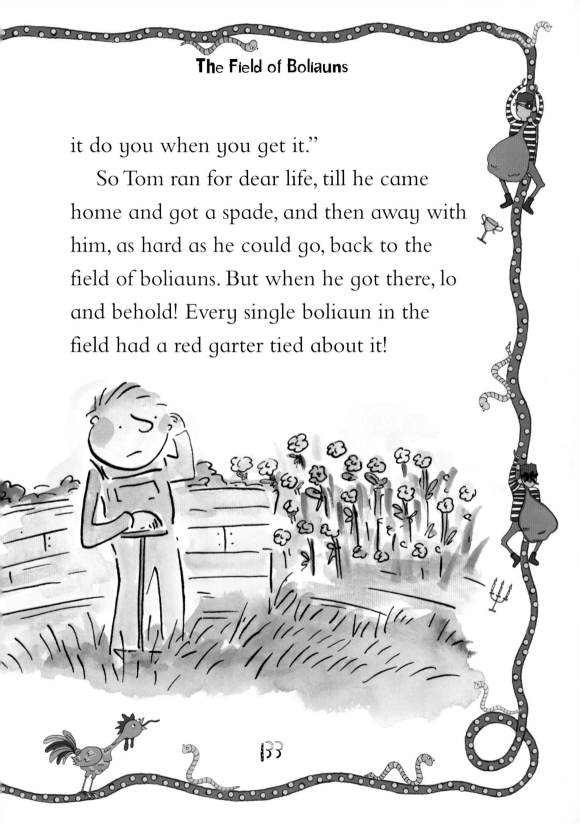

it do you when you get it."

So Tom ran for dear life, till he came home and got a spade, and then away with him, as hard as he could go, back to the field of boliauns. But when he got there, lo and behold! Every single boliaun in the field had a red garter tied about it!

"Whatever do I do now?" gasped Tom in exasperation. "I can't dig up the whole field, that's for sure—there's more than forty good Irish acres in it!"

So Tom came home again with his spade on his shoulder, a little cooler than he went, and many's the hearty curse he gave the Leprechaun every time he thought of the turn he had served him.

How the Dragon was Tricked

By Andrew Lang

Once upon a time there lived a man who had two sons, but the elder son hated the younger son. One day, as they were walking through a wood, the elder youth seized hold of the other, tied him to a tree, and went on his way hoping that his brother might starve to death.

However, it happened that an old and humpbacked shepherd passed by and said,

"Tell me, my son, why are you tied to that tree?"

"Because I was so crooked," answered the young man, "but it has quite cured me, and now my back is as straight as can be."

"I wish you would bind me to a tree," exclaimed the shepherd, "so that my back would get straight."

"With pleasure," replied the youth. "If you will loosen these cords I will tie you up as firmly as I can."

This was soon done, and then the young man drove off with the shepherd's sheep.

By these and many other tricks the young man soon became so famous that the King demanded to see him. Soldiers captured him and brought him before the

King, who said, "Because of your tricks and pranks, you should, in the eye of the law, be put to death. But if you can bring me the flying horse that belongs to the great dragon, I will spare you."

When night came the young man made his way straight to the dragon's home and the flying horse's stable. He was stretching his hand cautiously out to seize the bridle, when the horse suddenly began to neigh as loud as he could. This woke the sleeping dragon, who was very angry to be disturbed and came to give the horse a beating. The horse was very upset, and when the dragon returned back to bed, he let the young man lead him quietly away.

The King said, "The flying horse is all

very well, but I want something more. You must bring me the covering with the little bells that lies on the bed of the dragon, or I will have you put to death."

When night came the young man went away to the dragon's house and climbed up onto the roof. Then he opened a little window in the roof and let down a rope and tried to hook the bed covering to draw it up. But the little bells began to ring, and the dragon woke and drew the covering toward him, pulling the young man into the room as he did so. Then the dragon flung himself on the youth and bound him fast. He roared to his wife, saying, "Tomorrow when I go out you must stay at home and kill him and cook him. When I get back we

will eat him together."

So the following morning the dragoness took hold of the young man, and reached up on the shelf for a sharp knife with which to kill him. But as she untied the cords the better to get hold of him, the prisoner seized her and threw her into the oven. Then he snatched up the bed covering and carried it to the King.

"That is not enough," said His Majesty. "Bring me the dragon himself, or I will have you put to death."

"It shall be done," answered the youth, and he disguised himself as a beggar and set out on the road to the dragon's house. The young man found his enemy in front of his house, very busy making a box. "What is the box for?" inquired the beggar.

"It is for the man who killed my wife, and stole my flying horse and my bed covering," said the dragon.

"He deserves nothing better," answered the beggar. "Still that box doesn't look big enough for a man."

"You are wrong," said the dragon. "The box is large enough even for me."

"Well, of course, if you can get in, he should be able to," the man said. "But I am sure you would find it a tight fit."

"No, there is plenty of room," said the dragon, tucking himself carefully inside.

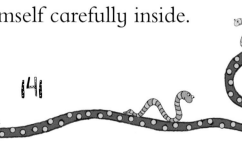

141

But no sooner was he well in, than the young man clapped the lid on tight, and drove in nails to make it tighter still. Then he took the box on his back and brought it to the King. When the King heard that the dragon was inside, he was so excited that he would not wait. He broke the lock and lifted the lid just a little way. The King was very careful not to leave enough space for the dragon to jump out, but unluckily there was just room for his great mouth.

With one snap the very foolish king vanished down his wide jaws. The young man married the King's daughter and ruled over the land, but what he did with the dragon nobody knows.

The Lad and the Devil

By Sir George Webbe Dasent

Once upon a time there was a lad who was walking along a road cracking nuts. He found one that was worm-eaten, and just at that very moment he met the Devil.

"Is it true, now," said the lad, "what they say, that the Devil can make himself as small as he chooses, and thrust himself in through a pinhole?"

"Yes, it is," said the Devil.

"Oh! It is, is it? Then let me see you do it, and just creep into this nut," said the lad.

So the Devil did it.

Now, when he had crept well into the nut through the worm's hole, the lad stopped it up with a pin. "Now, I've got you safe," he said, and put the nut in his pocket.

When he had walked on a bit, he came to a smithy. He turned in and asked the smith if he'd be good enough to crack that nut for him.

"Ay, that'll be an easy job," said the smith. He took his smallest hammer, laid the nut on the anvil and gave it a blow, but it wouldn't break.

So he took another hammer a little bigger, but that wasn't heavy enough either.

Then he took one bigger still, but it was still the same story, and so the smith got angry, and grasped his great sledgehammer.

"Now, I'll crack you to bits," he said, and let drive at the nut with all his might and main. And so the nut flew to pieces with a bang that blew off half the roof of the smithy, and the whole house creaked and groaned as though it were ready to fall.

"Why! The very Devil himself must have been in that nut," said the smith.

"So he was, you're quite right," said the lad, as he went away laughing.

The Endless Tale

By James Baldwin

Once upon a time in the Far East there was a great king who had no work to do. Every day and day long, he sat on cushions and listened to stories. No matter what the story was about, he never grew tired of hearing it, no matter how long it was.

"There is only one fault that I find with your story," he often said to the storyteller, "it is too short."

Eventually the King hit upon an idea. He sent out a proclamation saying that all the greatest storytellers in the world were invited to his palace. From far and wide they arrived, and some of them told tales that were very long indeed. But the King was always sad when a story came to an end.

At last he sent word into every city and town and country place, offering a prize to anyone who should tell him a tale that had no end at all—a tale that he could enjoy always. He said, "To the man that will tell me a story which shall last forever, I will give my fairest daughter for his wife, and I will make him my heir and he shall be king after me."

But this was not all. He added a very hard condition. "If any man shall try to tell such a story and then fail, he shall have his head cut off."

The King's daughter was very pretty, and there were many young men in that country who were willing to do anything to win her. But none of them wanted to lose their heads, so only a few tried for the prize.

One brave young man invented a story that lasted three months, but at the end of that time he could think of nothing more. His fate was a warning to others, and it was a long time before another storyteller was so rash as to try the King's patience.

But one day a stranger from the South came into the palace. "Great King," he said, "is it true that you offer a prize to the man who can tell a story that has no end?"

"It is true," said the King.

"And shall this man have your fairest daughter for his wife? Will he be your heir?"

"Yes, if he succeeds," said the King. "But if he fails, he shall lose his head."

"Very well, then," said the stranger. "I have a pleasant story about locusts which I would like to tell."

"Locusts?" remarked the King, his eyes gleaming with delight. "No one has ever told me a tale about locusts before. Do tell it," said the King. "I will gladly listen."

The storyteller began his tale.

"Once upon a time a king seized all the corn in his country, and stored it away in a strong granary. But a swarm of hungry locusts came over the land and saw where the grain had been put. After searching for many days they found on the east side of the granary a teeny-tiny crack that was just large enough for one locust to pass through at a time. So one locust went in and carried away a grain of corn, then another locust went in and carried away a grain of corn, then another locust went in and carried away a grain of corn. . ."

Day after day, week after week, the man kept on saying, "Then another locust went in and carried away a grain of corn…"

A month passed, a year passed, and still the man kept on saying, "Then another locust went in and carried away a grain of corn…"

At the end of two years, the King said, "How much longer will the locusts be going in and carrying away corn?"

"O King," said the storyteller, "they have as yet cleared only one cubit, and there are many thousand cubits in the granary."

"Man, man," cried the King, "you will drive me mad! I can listen to it no longer. Take my daughter, be my heir, rule my kingdom. But do not let me hear another word about those horrible locusts!"

And so it was that the strange storyteller married the King's daughter, and he lived happily in the land for many years. But his father-in-law, the King, did not care to listen to any more stories.

The Three Spinsters

By the Brothers Grimm

There was once a girl who was lazy and would not spin. No matter how her mother tried to persuade her to do it, she simply refused, point blank. At last the mother became angry and lost her patience, and gave the girl a beating so that she cried out loudly. At that moment the Queen was going by. As she heard the crying, she stopped. Going into the house, she asked the mother why she was beating her daughter so that everyone outside in the street could hear her cries.

The woman was ashamed to tell of her daughter's laziness, so she said, "I cannot stop her from spinning. She is forever at it, and I am poor and cannot furnish her with enough flax."

The Queen was delighted and answered, "I like nothing better than the sound of the spinning-wheel, and always feel happy when I hear its humming. Let me take your daughter with me to the castle—I have plenty of flax. She shall spin there to her heart's content."

The mother was only too glad of the

chance to get rid of her lazy, unhelpful daughter, and the Queen took the girl with her.

When they reached the castle, the Queen showed the girl three rooms that were filled with the finest flax, as full as they could hold. "Now you can spin me this flax," said the Queen, "and when you can show it to me all done you shall have my eldest son for your bridegroom. You may be poor, but I make nothing of that—if you prove yourself to be as hardworking as your mother led me to believe, that will be good enough for me."

The girl was inwardly terrified, for she could not have spun the flax even if she were to live to be a hundred years old, and were to sit spinning every day of her life from morning to evening. When she found herself alone she began to weep, and sat so for three days without putting her hand to the spinning-wheel.

On the third day the Queen came, and when she saw that nothing had been done of the spinning she was much surprised. The girl excused herself by saying that she had not been able to begin because of the distress she was in at leaving her home and her mother. The excuse contented the Queen, who said, as she went away, "Tomorrow you must begin to work."

When the girl found herself alone again she could not tell how to help herself or what to do, and in her upset she went and gazed out of the window. There she saw three women passing by. The first of them had a broad flat foot, the second had a big under-lip that hung down over her chin, and the third had a remarkably broad thumb. They all of them stopped in front of the window, and called out to know what it was that the girl wanted. She told them about the awful situation she found herself in. The girl couldn't believe her ears when the three ugly women promised her their help, and said, "Then will you invite us to your wedding, and not be ashamed of us, and call us your cousins, and let us sit at your table? If you will promise this, we will finish off your flax-spinning in a very short time."

"With all my heart," answered the girl, "only come in now, and begin at once." Of course, she would have promised them anything at all to have the spinning done in time to show the Queen!

Then these same women came in, and she cleared a space in the first room for them to sit and begin their spinning. The first one drew out the thread and moved the treaddle that turned the wheel. The second moistened the thread. The third twisted it and rapped with her finger on the table, and as often as she rapped, a heap of yarn fell to the ground, and it was most beautifully spun.

The girl hid the three spinsters out of the Queen's sight, and only showed her, as often as she came, the heaps of well-spun yarn. There was no end to the praises she received. When the first room was empty the women went on to the second, and then to the third, so that at last all of the flax had been spun.

Then the three women took their leave,

saying to the girl, "Do not forget what you have promised and it will be all the better for you."

So when the girl took the Queen and showed her the empty rooms and the great heaps of yarn, the wedding was at once arranged. The bridegroom rejoiced that he should have so clever and hardworking a wife, and praised her exceedingly.

"I have three cousins," said the girl, "and as they have shown me a great deal of kindness, I would not wish to forget them in my good fortune. May I be allowed to invite them to the wedding, and to ask them to sit at the table with us?"

The Queen and the bridegroom said at once, "Of course."

So when the feast began, in came the three spinsters in strange guise, and the bride said, "Dear cousins, you are welcome."

"Oh," said the bridegroom, "how did you come to have such dreadfully ugly relations?" Then he went up to the first spinster and said, "How is it that you have such a broad flat foot?"

"With treading," answered she, "with treading."

Then he went up to the second and said, "How is it that you have such a great hanging lip?"

"With licking," answered she, "with licking."

Then he asked the third, "How is it that you have such a broad thumb?"

"With twisting thread," answered she,

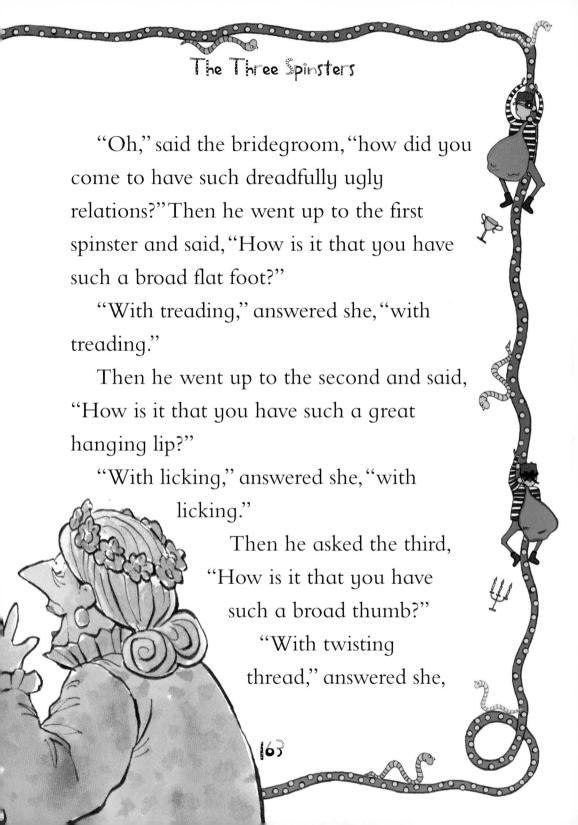

165

"with twisting thread."

Then the bridegroom said that from that time forward his beautiful bride should never touch a spinning-wheel.

And so she escaped that tiresome flax-spinning once and for all.

The Stone Soup

A folk tale

Many years ago three soldiers were on their way home from war, hungry and weary of battle, when they came upon a small village. The villagers had suffered a poor harvest because so many of them had been called away to fight. They quickly hid what little food they had and met the three strangers in the village square, moaning about how starving they all were.

The first
soldier said to the villagers,
"Your tired fields have left you nothing
to share. We will share what little we have—
the secret of how to make soup from stones."

A murmur of excitement rippled through
the crowd. Soon a fire was put to the town's
greatest pot. Everyone watched with
curiosity as the soldiers dropped in three
stones. "Now this will be a fine soup," said

the second soldier, "but a pinch of salt and
some parsley would make it wonderful!"
Up jumped a villager, crying, "I've
just remembered where some is!"

She returned
with an apronful of parsley
and a turnip to boot.
The memory of the villagers strangely
seemed to improve. Soon barley, carrots,

beef, and cream had found their way into the great pot, and even a cask of wine was rolled into the square.

It didn't seem long before everyone was sitting down to a delicious-smelling, rich soup, packed with tasty, chunky vegetables.

The villagers ate and danced and sang well into the night, refreshed by the feast and their new-found friends. They couldn't remember when they had last had such an enjoyable meal. It was the early hours of the morning before everyone finally turned in to bed.

When the three soldiers awoke they found the entire village standing before them. At their feet lay a satchel of the village's best breads and cheese. "You have given us the greatest of gifts—the secret of how to make soup from stones," said an elder, "and we shall never forget."

The third soldier turned to the crowd, and said, "There is no secret, but this is certain—it is only by sharing that we may make a feast."

And off the soldiers wandered down the road, leaving the villagers bewildered but thoughtful behind them.

Which was the Foolishest?

By Andrew Lang

In a little village that stood on a wide plain, where you could see the sun from the moment he rose to the moment he set, there lived two couples side by side. The men, who both worked under the same master, were good friends, but the wives were always quarreling, and the subject they quarreled most about was which of the two had the stupidest husband. Each woman

thought her own husband the more foolish
of the two.

"You should just see what he does!" one
woman said to her neighbor. "When he
dresses the baby, he puts her frock on upside
down, and, one day, I found him trying to
feed her with boiling hot soup. Then he
picks up stones in the road and sows them
instead of potatoes, and one day he wanted
to go into the garden from the top window,
because he declared it was a shorter way
than through the door."

"That is bad enough, of course,"
answered the other, "but it is really nothing
to what I have to endure every day from
my husband. If, when I am busy, I ask him
to go and feed the hens, he is certain to give

them some poisonous stuff instead of their proper food, and when I visit the yard next I find them all dead. Once, when I had gone away to my sick mother, he even took my best bonnet, and when I came back I found he had given it to the hen to lay her eggs in. And you know that, only last week, when I sent him to buy a cask of butter he returned driving a hundred and fifty ducks that someone had persuaded him to take. And not one of them would lay!"

"Yes, I am afraid he is trying," replied the first, "but let us put them to the test, and see which of them is the most foolish."

So, about the time that she expected her husband home from work, the first wife got out her spinning-wheel, and sat busily turning it, taking care not even to look up from her work when the man came in. For some minutes he stood with his mouth open watching her, and as she still remained silent, he said at last, "Have you gone mad, wife, that you sit spinning without anything on the wheel?"

"You may think that there is nothing on it," answered she, "but I can assure you that there is a large skein of wool, so fine that nobody can see it, which will be woven into a coat for you."

175

"Dear me!" he replied. "What a clever wife I have got! If you had not told me I should never have known that there was any wool on the wheel at all. But now I really do seem to see something."

The woman smiled and was silent, and after spinning busily for an hour more, she got up from her stool, and began to weave as fast as she could. At last she got up, and said to her husband, "I am too tired to finish it tonight, so I shall go to bed, and tomorrow I shall only have the cutting and stitching to do."

So the next morning she got up early, and after she had cleaned her house, and fed her chickens, and put everything in its place again, she bent over the kitchen table, and the sound of her big scissors could be heard *snip! snap!* as far as the garden. Her husband could not see anything to snip at, but then he was so stupid that this was not very surprising!

After the cutting came the sewing. The woman patted and pinned and fixed and joined. Then she turned to her husband and said, "Now it is ready for you to try on." She made him take off his coat and stand up in front of her. Then, once more, she patted and pinned and fixed and joined, and was very careful in smoothing out every wrinkle.

"It does not feel very warm," observed the man at last, when he had put up with all this patiently for a long time.

175

"That is because it is so fine," answered she, "you do not want it to be as thick as the rough clothes you wear every day."

He did but was ashamed to say so, and only answered, "Well, I am sure it must be beautiful since you say so, and I shall be smarter than anyone in the whole village. 'Oh, what a splendid coat!' they will exclaim when they see me walk by. But it is not everybody who has a wife as clever as mine."

Meanwhile, the other wife was not idle. As soon as her husband entered she stared at him with such a look of terror that the poor man was quite frightened.

"Why do you stare at me so? Is there anything the matter?" he asked.

176

"Oh! Go to bed at once," she cried. "You must be very ill indeed to look like that!"

The man was rather surprised at first, as he felt particularly well that evening, but the moment his wife spoke he became quite certain that he had something dreadful the matter with him, and grew quite pale.

"I dare say it would be the best place for me," he answered, trembling, and he asked his wife to take him upstairs and help him change into his night clothes.

"If you sleep well during the night there may be a chance for you," said she, shaking her head, as she tucked him up warmly, "but if not…"

Of course the poor man never closed an eye till the sun rose.

177

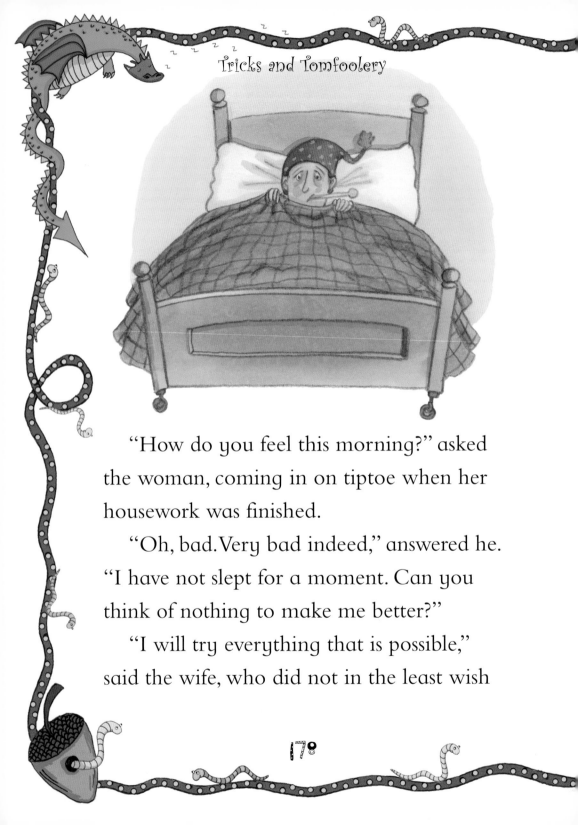

"How do you feel this morning?" asked the woman, coming in on tiptoe when her housework was finished.

"Oh, bad. Very bad indeed," answered he. "I have not slept for a moment. Can you think of nothing to make me better?"

"I will try everything that is possible," said the wife, who did not in the least wish her husband to die, but was determined to show that he was more foolish than the other man. "I will get some dried herbs and make you a drink, but I am very much afraid that it is too late. Why did you not tell me before?"

"I thought perhaps the pain would go off in a day or two, and besides, I did not want to make you unhappy," answered the man, who was by this time quite sure he had been suffering tortures, and had put up with them like a hero. "Of course, if I had had any idea how ill I really was, I would have spoken at once."

"Well, well, I will see what can be done," said the wife, "but talking is not good for you. Lie still and keep yourself warm."

All that day the man lay in bed, and whenever his wife entered the room and asked him, with a shake of the head, how he felt, he always replied that he was getting worse. At last, in the evening, she burst into tears, and when he inquired what was the matter, she sobbed out, "Oh, my poor, poor husband, are you really dead? I must go tomorrow and order your coffin."

Now, when the man heard this, a cold shiver ran through his body, and all at once he knew that he was as well as he had ever been in his life.

"Oh, no, no!" he cried. "I feel quite recovered! Indeed, I think I shall go out to work."

"You will do no such thing," replied his

wife. "Just keep quite quiet, for before the sun rises you will be a dead man."

The man was very frightened at her words, and lay absolutely still while the undertaker came and measured him for his coffin, while his wife gave orders to the gravedigger about his grave.

That evening the coffin was sent to their home. In the morning at nine o'clock the woman dressed him in a long flannel robe, and called the undertaker's men to fasten down the lid and carry him to the grave, where all their friends were waiting for them.

Just as the body was being placed in the ground the other woman's husband came running up, dressed—as far as anyone could see—in no clothes at all. Everybody burst into shouts of laughter at the sight of him, and the men laid down the coffin and laughed too, till their sides nearly split. The dead man was so astonished at this behavior that he peeped out of a little window in the side of the coffin, and cried out, "I should laugh as loudly as any of you, if I were not a dead man."

When they heard the voice coming from the coffin the other people stopped laughing, and stood as if they had been turned into stone. They rushed to the coffin and lifted the lid so that the man could step out.

"Were you really not dead after all?" asked they. "And if not, why did you let yourself be buried?"

At this the wives confessed that they had each wished to prove that her husband was stupider than the other. But the villagers declared that they could not decide which was the most foolish.

So the women quarreled just as much as they did before, and no one ever knew whose husband was the most foolish.

Wishing for Wings

An extract from *Five Children and It*
by E. Nesbit

Five children—Cyril, Anthea, Robert, Jane, and the youngest, a baby whom they call "the Lamb"—move house from London to the countryside in Kent. In a gravel pit behind their home, they discover a strange creature called a Psammead, or Sand-fairy. He is able to grant one wish per day, and, over the next three days, he grants the children their wishes to become beautiful, to have heaps of gold coins, and for the Psammead to be wanted by everyone. Each foolish wish causes the children to run into trouble. Fortunately, every day the Psammead's magic lasts only till sunset…

Have you ever been up at five o'clock on a fine summer morning? It is very beautiful. The sunlight is pinky and yellowy, and all the grass and trees are covered with dew-diamonds. All the shadows go the opposite way to the way they do in the evening, which is very interesting and makes you feel as though you were in a new other world.

Anthea awoke at five. She had made herself wake, and I must tell you how it is done, even if it keeps you waiting for the story to go on.

You get into bed at night, and lie down quite flat on your little back with your hands straight down by your sides. Then you say "I must wake up at five" (or six, or seven, or eight, or nine, or whatever the time is that you want), and as you say it you push your chin down on to your chest and then bang your head back on the pillow.

And you do this as many times as there are ones in the time you want to wake up at. (It is quite an easy sum.) Of course everything depends on your really wanting to get up at five (or six, or seven, or eight, or nine). If you don't really want to, it's all of no use. But if you do—well, try it and see. Of course in this, as in doing Latin prose or getting into mischief, practice makes perfect. Anthea was quite perfect.

At the very moment when she opened her eyes, Anthea heard the black-and-gold clock down in the dining room strike eleven. So she knew it was three minutes to five. The black-and-gold clock always struck wrong, but it was all right when you knew what it meant. It was like a person talking a foreign language. If you know the language it is just as easy to understand as English. And Anthea knew the clock language.

She was very sleepy, but she jumped out of bed and put her face and hands into a basin of cold water. This is a fairy charm that prevents your wanting to get back into bed again. Then she dressed, and folded up her nightgown. She did not tumble it together by

187

the sleeves, but instead folded it by the seams from the hem, and that will show you the kind of well brought-up little girl she was.

Then Anthea took her shoes in her hand and crept softly down the stairs. She opened the dining room window and climbed out. It would have been just as easy to go out by the door, but the window was more romantic, and less likely to be noticed by Martha, the nanny.

"I will always get up at five," Anthea said to herself. "It is quite too awfully pretty for anything."

Her heart was beating very fast, for she was carrying out a plan quite her own. She could not be sure that it was a good plan, but she was quite sure that it would not be any better if she were to tell the others about it. And she had a feeling that, right or wrong, she would rather go through with it alone.

Anthea put on her shoes under the iron veranda, on the red and yellow shining tiles. Then she ran straight to the gravel pit. She quickly found the Psammead's place and dug it out.

It was very cross indeed.

"It's too bad," it said, fluffing up its fur like pigeons do their feathers at Christmas time. "The weather's arctic, and it's the middle of the night."

"I'm so sorry," said Anthea gently. She took off her white pinafore and covered the

Sand-fairy up with it, all but its head, its bat's ears, and its eyes that were like a snail's eyes.

"Thank you," it said, "that's better. What's the wish this morning?"

"I don't know," said she, "that's just it. You see, we've been very unlucky so far. I wanted to talk to you about it. But—would you mind not giving me any wishes till after breakfast? It's so hard to talk to anyone if they jump out at you with wishes you don't really want!"

"You shouldn't say you wish for things if you don't wish for them."

"I'll try not to," said Anthea, "but I do wish—"

"Look out!" said the Psammead in a

warning voice, and it began to blow itself out.

"Oh, this isn't a magic wish—it's just—I should be so glad if you'd not swell yourself out and nearly burst to give me anything just now. Wait till the others are here."

"Well, well," it said indulgently, but it shivered.

"Would you like to come and sit on my lap?" asked Anthea kindly. "You'd be warmer, and I could turn the skirt of my frock up round you. I'd be very careful."

Anthea had never expected that it would, but it did.

"Thank you," it said, "you really are rather thoughtful." It crept on to her lap and snuggled down, and she put her arms

191

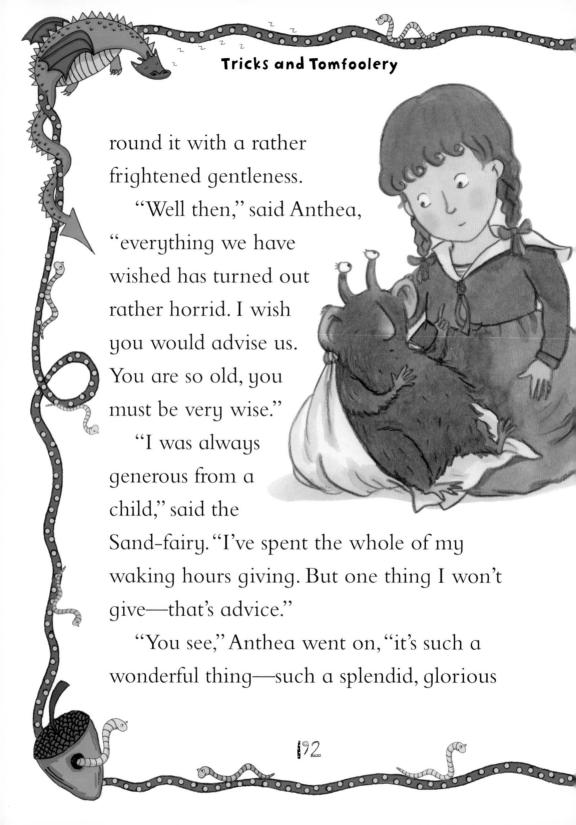

round it with a rather frightened gentleness.

"Well then," said Anthea, "everything we have wished has turned out rather horrid. I wish you would advise us. You are so old, you must be very wise."

"I was always generous from a child," said the Sand-fairy. "I've spent the whole of my waking hours giving. But one thing I won't give—that's advice."

"You see," Anthea went on, "it's such a wonderful thing—such a splendid, glorious

chance. It's so good and kind and dear of
you to give us our wishes, and it seems such
a pity it should all be wasted just because
we are too silly to know what to wish for."

Anthea had meant to say that—and she
had not wanted to say it before the others.
It's one thing to say you're silly, and quite
another to say that other people are.

"Child," said the Sand-fairy sleepily,
"I can only advise you to think before
you speak…"

"But I thought you never gave advice."

"That piece doesn't count," it said.
"You'll never take it! Besides, it's not
original. It's in all the copy books."

"But won't you just say if you think
wings would be a silly wish?"

"Wings?" it said. "I should think you might do worse. Only, take care you aren't flying high at sunset. There was a little Ninevite boy I heard of once. He was one of King Sennacherib's sons, and a traveler brought him a Psammead. He used to keep it in a box of sand on the palace terrace. It was a dreadful degradation for one of us, of course. Still, the boy was the Assyrian King's son.

"One day," continued the Sand-fairy, "he wished for wings and got them. But at sunset, the wings turned into stone, and he fell slap onto one of the winged lions at the top of his father's great staircase, and what with *his* stone wings and the lion's stone wings—well, it's not a pretty story! But I

believe the boy enjoyed himself very much
till then… Goodbye. I *am* so sleepy."

It jumped off her lap, dug frantically,
and vanished.

Anthea was late for breakfast. Afterward,
she and the others went back to the gravel
pit, without the Lamb. In the lane Anthea,
breathless from scurrying about, panted out,
"I want to propose we take turns to wish.
Only, nobody's to have a wish if the others
don't think it's a nice wish. Do you agree?"

"Who's to have first wish?" asked Robert
cautiously.

"Me, if you don't mind," said Anthea
apologetically. "And I've thought about it—
and it's wings."

There was a silence. The others rather wanted to find fault, but it was hard because the word "wings" raised a flutter of joyous excitement in every breast.

"Not so dusty," said Cyril generously, and Robert added, "Really, Panther, you're not quite such a fool as you look."

Jane said, "I think it would be perfectly lovely. It's like a bright, joyful dream."

They found the Sand-fairy easily.

Anthea said, "I wish we all had beautiful wings to fly with."

The Sand-fairy blew himself out, and next moment each child felt a funny feeling, half heaviness and half lightness, on its shoulders.

Then the Psammead put its head on one

side and turned its snail's eyes from one child to the other. "Not so dusty," it said dreamily. "But really, Robert, you're not quite such an angel as you look." Robert almost blushed.

The wings were very big, and more beautiful than you can possibly imagine— for they were soft and smooth, and every feather lay neatly in its place. And the feathers were of the most lovely mixed changing colors, like the rainbow, or iridescent glass, or the beautiful scum that sometimes floats on water that is not at all nice to drink.

"Oh—but can we fly?" Jane said, standing anxiously, first on one foot and then on the other.

"Look out!" said Cyril. "You're treading on my wing."

"Does it hurt?" asked Anthea with interest, but no one answered, for Robert had spread his wings and jumped up, and now he was slowly rising in the air. He looked very awkward in his knickerbocker suit—his boots in particular hung helplessly, and seemed much larger than when he was standing in them. But the others cared little how he looked—or how they looked, for that matter. For now they all spread out their

wings and rose in the air.
Of course you all know
what flying feels like
because everyone has
dreamed about flying, and it seems
so beautifully easy—only, you can
never remember how you did it. As
a rule you have
to do it without
wings in your
dreams, which is
more clever and
uncommon, but not so
easy to remember the rule for.
Now the four children rose
flapping from the ground, and you can't
think how good the air felt running

against their faces. Their wings were tremendously wide when they were spread out, and they had to fly quite a long way apart so as not to get in each other's way. But little things like this are easily learned.

All the words in the English Dictionary, and in the Greek Lexicon as well, are, I find, of no use at all to tell you exactly what it feels like to be flying, so I will not try. But I will say that to look down on the fields and woods, instead of along at them, is something like looking at a beautiful live map, where, instead of silly colors on paper, you have real moving sunny woods and green fields laid out one after the other. As Cyril said, and I can't think where he got hold of such a strange expression, "It does

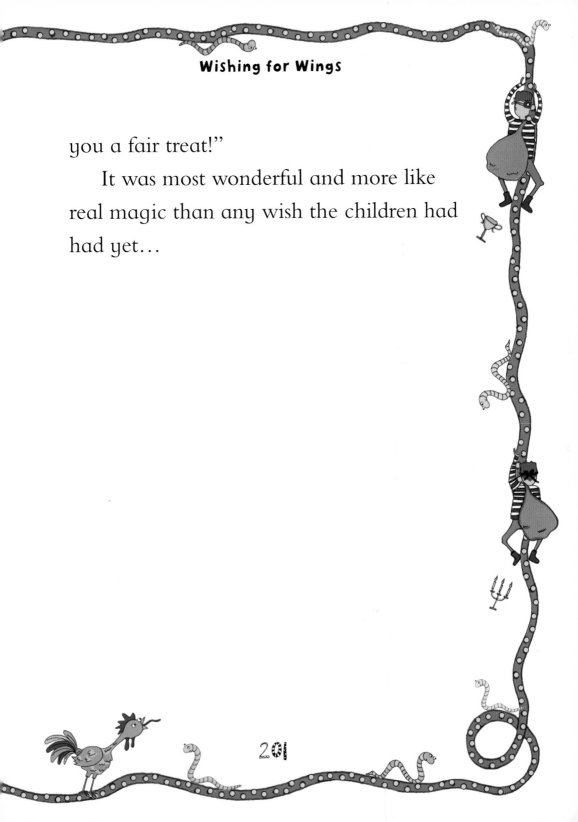

you a fair treat!"

It was most wonderful and more like real magic than any wish the children had had yet…

The Greedy Brownie

Edited by Hamilton Wright Mabie,
Edward Everett Hale, and
William Byron Forbush

There was once a little Brownie who lived in a hollow tree stump. He had been busy all the day playing pranks, as all Brownies love to do. His pranks had taken him far away from home to the house of a very important landowner, or laird. Into the laird's cup of wine the Brownie had dropped some horribly sour berries, which he had picked on his way. The Brownie also put prickly thistles into the laird's boots, so that when he had drawn them on he had screamed out with pain.

The Brownie had been away all the day, so when at last he turned to go back to his home he felt really very tired. On his way back to the wood he passed by a cosy-looking farmhouse. The door of the dairy was open. The Brownie thought this would be a very nice cool place in which to rest for a few moments. So he slipped into the dairy and curled himself up underneath the bench to have a nice little doze.

He was so weary that once he had fallen asleep he never woke up again until it was quite dark. He was disturbed by two lassies

who had come into the dairy. One was
carrying a candle, and by its light the pair
spied a big bowl of cream on the shelf. The
naughty girls thought that they would
drink it for supper. They could only find one
spoon on the shelf, so they decided they
would each have a spoonful in turn.

Lassie Jean carried the bowl to a bench
in the corner, and Lassie Meg followed with
the candle. No sooner had the two girls
settled themselves than the Brownie, who
was now wide awake and feeling that some
supper might not be out of place, crept up
behind them and blew out the candle.

The lassies at first were very concerned
at being in the dark. Nevertheless, they
determined they would drink the cream

all the same. Lassie Jean filled the spoon
with the rich delicacy. She was about to
raise it to her lips when the naughty
Brownie poked his head over her shoulder,
and lapped it out of
the spoon before
it had reached
her mouth.

Lassie Meg, believing that Lassie Jean had already swallowed some cream while she had had none, stretched out her hand to take away the spoon from her friend. Lassie Jean was not willing to give it up, since she said she had not yet tasted any cream.

Lassie Meg was unwilling to believe her, for she declared she had heard her lapping the cream. Without waiting for Lassie Jean to explain, she snatched the spoon from her friend's hand. She filled it with cream from the bowl, and was about to raise it to her lips when the Brownie jumped from behind Lassie Jean, and settled himself behind the shoulders of Lassie Meg. He poked forward his head, and again lapped up the cream from out of the spoon. Lassie Jean, in her

turn, snatched back the spoon from
Lassie Meg…

Thus they went on, for every time one
or the other raised the spoonful of cream
to her lips it was lapped up by the gleeful
Brownie. This continued until the bowl was
emptied. The Brownie was full of cream and
quite drunk with happiness, but the lassies
had not tasted one drop, although each
believed the other had drunk it all.

The foolish lassies were still quarreling
when the door of the dairy was opened,
and the farmer's wife entered, carrying a
lighted candle in her hand. The moment
that she did so the tricksy Brownie hopped
underneath the bench, and the lassies
started up guiltily.

At once, the farmer's wife caught sight of the empty basin. She was very angry with the two girls indeed. When they tried hastily to explain, each blaming the other, the farmer's wife would not listen, but only grew the more angry. She told them that, since they had supped so well, they should have none of the scones and eggs which she had prepared for the evening meal.

When the farmer's wife had entered she had left the door open, so while she was busily scolding the lassies the naughty Brownie slipped out from under the bench and made his escape. As he ran chuckling down the road, he could still hear the farmer's wife's angry voice drowning the explanations of the bewildered lassies.

When the little fellow curled himself up some time later in the tree trunk he was still laughing.

Sillies and Simpletons

Mr. Vinegar

By Joseph Jacobs

Mr. and Mrs. Vinegar lived in a vinegar bottle. Now, one day, when Mr. Vinegar was away from home, Mrs. Vinegar (who was a very good housewife) was busily sweeping her house when an unlucky thump of the broom brought the whole house clitter-clatter, clitter-clatter about her ears. In an agony of grief she rushed forth to meet her husband.

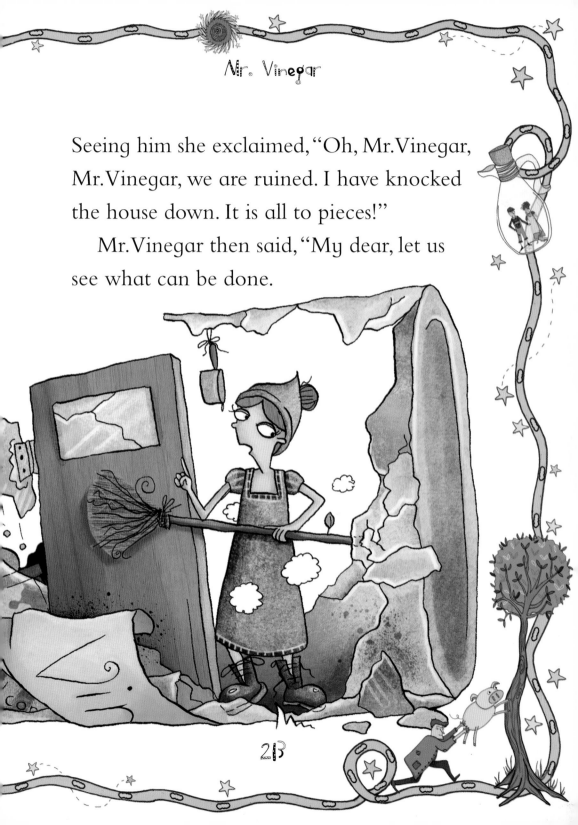

Seeing him she exclaimed, "Oh, Mr. Vinegar, Mr. Vinegar, we are ruined. I have knocked the house down. It is all to pieces!"

Mr. Vinegar then said, "My dear, let us see what can be done.

Here is the door—I will take it on my back, and we will go forth to seek our fortune."

They walked all that day, and at nightfall entered a thick forest. They were both very, very tired, and Mr. Vinegar said, "My love, I will climb up into a tree, drag up the door, and you shall follow." He accordingly did so, and they both stretched their weary limbs on the door and fell fast asleep.

In the middle of the night Mr. Vinegar was disturbed by the sound of voices underneath, and to his horror and dismay found that it was a band of thieves met to divide their booty.

"Here, Jack," said one, "here's five coins for you. Bill, here's ten coins for you. Bob, here's three coins for you."

Mr. Vinegar could listen no longer. His terror was so great that he trembled and trembled, and shook down the door on their heads. Away scampered the thieves, but Mr. Vinegar dared not leave his hiding place till broad daylight.

He then scrambled out of the tree and went to lift up the door. What did he see, but a number of golden coins. "Come down, Mrs. Vinegar," he cried. "Come down, I say. Our fortune's made, our fortune's made! Come down, I say."

Mrs. Vinegar climbed down as fast as she could, and when she saw the money she jumped for joy. "Now, my dear," said she, "I'll tell you what you shall do. There is a fair at the neighboring town—you shall take these forty coins and buy a cow. I can make butter and cheese, which you shall sell at the market, and we shall then be able to live very comfortably."

Mr. Vinegar joyfully agreed. He took the money, and off he went to the fair. When he arrived he walked up and down, and at length saw a beautiful red cow. It was an excellent milker, and perfect in every way. 'Oh,' thought Mr. Vinegar, 'if I had but that cow, I should be the happiest man alive.'

So he offered the forty coins for the cow, and the owner said that, as he was a friend, he'd oblige him. So the bargain was made and Mr. Vinegar got the cow, and he drove it backward and forward to show it.

By and by he saw a man playing the bagpipes, *tweedle-dum tweedle-dee*. The children followed him about, and he appeared to be pocketing money on all sides. 'Well,' thought Mr. Vinegar, 'if I had but that beautiful instrument, I should be the happiest man alive—my fortune would be made.'

So Mr. Vinegar went up to the man. "Friend," said he, "what a beautiful instrument that is, and what a deal of money you must make."

"Why, yes," said the man, "I make a great deal of money, to be sure, and it is a wonderful instrument."

"Oh!" cried Mr. Vinegar, "how I should like to possess it!"

217

"Well," said the man, "as you are a friend, I don't much mind parting with it. You shall have it for that red cow."

"Done!" said the delighted Mr. Vinegar. So the red cow was given for the bagpipes.

He walked up and down with his purchase, but it was in vain he tried to play a tune. Instead of pocketing pence, boys followed him hooting, laughing, and throwing things.

Poor Mr. Vinegar. His fingers grew very cold, and,

just as he was leaving the town, he met
a man with a fine thick pair of gloves.
"Oh, my fingers are so very cold," said
Mr. Vinegar to himself. "Now if I had but
those beautiful gloves, I should be the
happiest man alive." He went up to the
man, and said to him, "Friend, you seem to
have a capital pair of gloves there."

"Yes, truly," cried the man, "and my
hands are as warm as possible this cold
November day."

"Well," said Mr. Vinegar, "I should like to
have them."

"What will you give?" said the man. "As
you are a friend, I don't much mind letting
you have them for those bagpipes."

"Done!" cried Mr. Vinegar. He put on

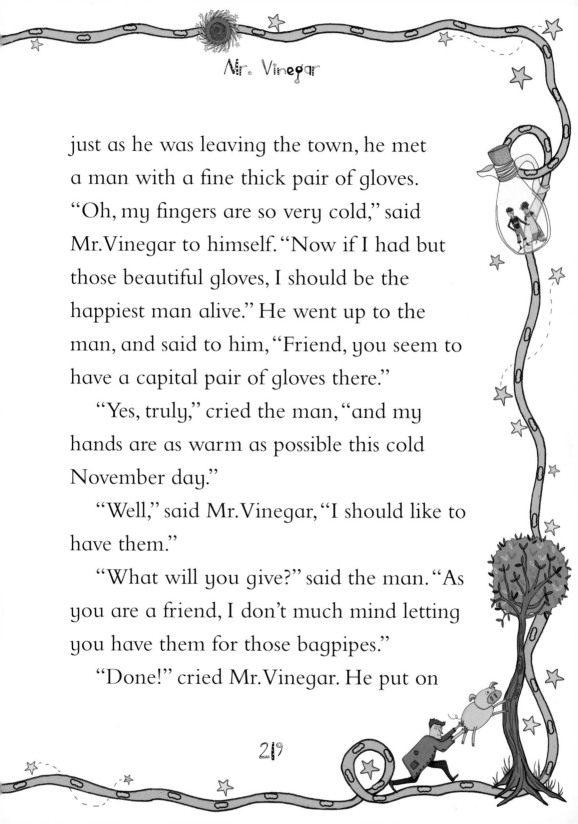

the gloves and felt perfectly happy as he trudged homeward.

At last he grew very tired, when he saw a man coming toward him with a good stout walking stick in his hand. "Oh," said Mr. Vinegar, "that I had but that stick! I should then be the happiest man alive." He said to the man: "Friend! What a rare good stick you have got."

"Yes," said the man, "I have used it for many a long mile, and a good friend it has been. But if you have a fancy for it, as you are a friend, I don't mind giving it to you for that pair of gloves."

Mr. Vinegar's hands were so warm, and his legs so tired, that he gladly made the exchange.

As he drew near to the wood where he had left his wife, he heard a parrot in a tree calling out his name.

"Mr. Vinegar, you foolish man, you blockhead, you simpleton," mocked the parrot. "You went to the fair, and laid out all your money in buying a cow. Not content with that, you changed it for bagpipes, on which you could not play, and which were not worth one-tenth of the money. You had no sooner got the bagpipes than you changed them for gloves, which were not worth one-quarter of the money. And when you had got the gloves, you changed them for a poor miserable stick. And now for your forty coins, cow, bagpipes, and gloves, you have nothing to

221

show but that
miserable stick,
which you might
have cut in a hedge."
On this the bird
laughed, and
Mr. Vinegar, falling
into a violent rage,
threw the stick at its
head. The stick
lodged in the tree,
and he returned to his wife without money,
cow, bagpipes, gloves, or stick. She instantly
gave him such a sound scolding that he
never did anything quite so silly again.

The Moon-Cake

Edited by Hamilton Wright Mabie,
Edward Everett Hale, and
William Byron Forbush

A little boy had a cake that a big boy really wanted for himself. The greedy lad thought hard, wondering how he could get the cake without making the little boy cry, for then surely it would attract his mother's attention and she would see what was going on. Just in time, as the little boy held up the cake to his lips to take a bite, the big boy hit on an idea.

"How much prettier that cake would be if it were more like the moon!" he remarked.

The little boy stopped, his mouth open wide, and examined the tasty morsel in his hand. 'Surely something that looked like the moon would indeed be prettier,' he thought to himself.

Seeing the little boy's hesitation, the big boy seized the chance to press on. "I can make it look like the moon," he promised, "I have done it many times before."

"Really?" asked the little boy. "Honest?"

"Of course," replied the big boy, with a smirk, "hand it over."

No sooner had the little boy handed over his delicious-looking cake than the big boy took out a mouthful, leaving a crescent with a jagged edge.

"Nooooooo!" cried out the little boy, beginning to whimper and trying to grab back the cake.

Holding it out of his reach the big boy hastily urged, "Don't worry—I'll make it better. I'll neaten it up into a half-moon." So saying, he nibbled off the horns of the crescent, and gnawed the edge smooth.

But when the half-moon was made, the little boy saw that there was hardly any cake left, and he began to wail. The big boy again interrupted, telling him that, if he did not like so small a moon, he should have one that was just the size of the real thing. He then took the cake, and explained that, just before the new moon is seen, the old moon disappears. Then he swallowed the rest of the cake and ran off, leaving the little boy waiting for the new moon.

The Remarkable Rocket

By Oscar Wilde

The King's son was going to be married,
so there was great rejoicing. He had waited
a whole year for his bride, and at last she
had arrived. She was a Russian princess,
and had driven all the way from Finland in
a sledge drawn by six reindeer. The sledge
was shaped like a great golden swan, and
between the swan's wings lay the Princess
herself. Her long ermine cloak reached

down to her feet, on her head was a tiny silver cap, and she was as pale as the Snow Palace in which she had always lived. As she drove through the streets all the people threw down flowers on her from the balconies.

At the gate of the castle the Prince was waiting to receive her. When he saw her he sank upon one knee, and kissed her hand. "Your picture was beautiful," he murmured, "but you are more beautiful than your picture." The Princess blushed.

When the day for the marriage arrived, it was a magnificent ceremony. The bride and bridegroom walked hand in hand under a canopy of purple velvet embroidered with little pearls. Then there was a state banquet, which lasted for five hours. The Prince and Princess sat at the top of the Great Hall and drank out of a cup of clear crystal.

After the banquet there was a ball. The bride and bridegroom were to dance the Rose-dance together, and the King played the flute. He played very badly, but no one dared to tell him so because he was the King. Indeed, everybody cried out, "Charming! Charming!"

The last item on the program was a grand display of fireworks, to be let off exactly at midnight. The little Princess had never seen a firework in her life and was most excited. At the end of the King's garden a great stand had been set up. As soon as everything had been put in its proper place, the fireworks began to talk to each other.

"The world is certainly very beautiful," cried a little Squib. "Just look at those yellow tulips. Why! If they were real crackers they could not be lovelier. I am very glad I have traveled. Travel improves the mind wonderfully."

"The King's garden is not the world, you foolish squib," said a big Roman Candle. "The world is an enormous place, and it would take you three days to see it all."

"Any place you love is the world to you," said a thoughtful Catharine Wheel.

Suddenly, a sharp, dry cough was heard, and they all looked round.

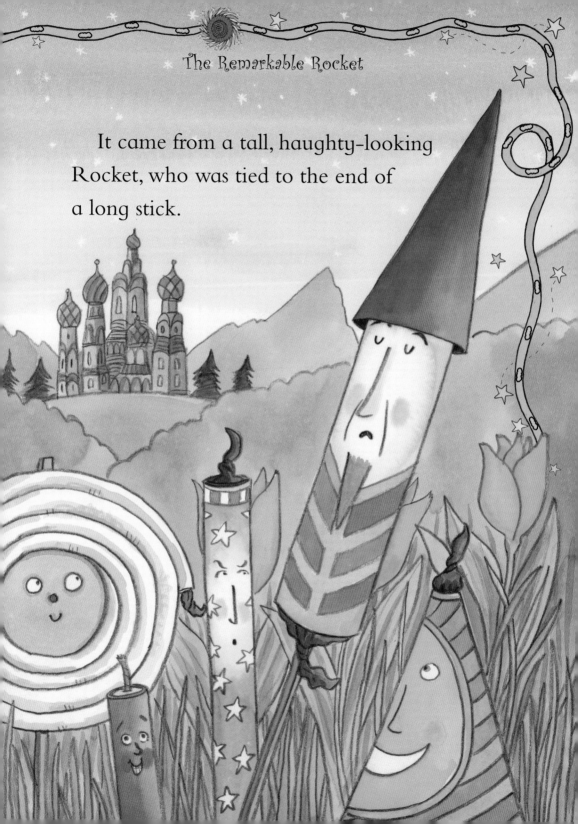

It came from a tall, haughty-looking Rocket, who was tied to the end of a long stick.

"Ahem! Ahem!" he said again. Then he spoke in a very distinguished manner. "How fortunate it is for the King's son," he remarked, "that he is to be married on the very day on which I am to be let off. Really, if it had been arranged beforehand, it could not have turned out better for him, but princes are always lucky."

"Dear me!" said the little Squib. "I thought it was quite the other way, and that we were to be let off in the Prince's honor."

"It may be so with you," he answered. "Indeed, I have no doubt that it is, but with me it is different. I am a very remarkable Rocket, and come of remarkable parents. My mother was the most celebrated

Catharine Wheel of her day, and was renowned for her graceful dancing. When she made her great public appearance she span round nineteen times before she went out, and each time that she did so she threw into the air seven pink stars. She was three feet and a half across, and made of the very best gunpowder.

"My father was a Rocket like myself," continued the Rocket, "and from French grandparents. He flew so high that the people were afraid that he would never come down again. He did though, and he made a most brilliant descent in a shower of golden rain. The newspapers wrote about his performance in very flattering terms. The *Court Gazette* called him a triumph!"

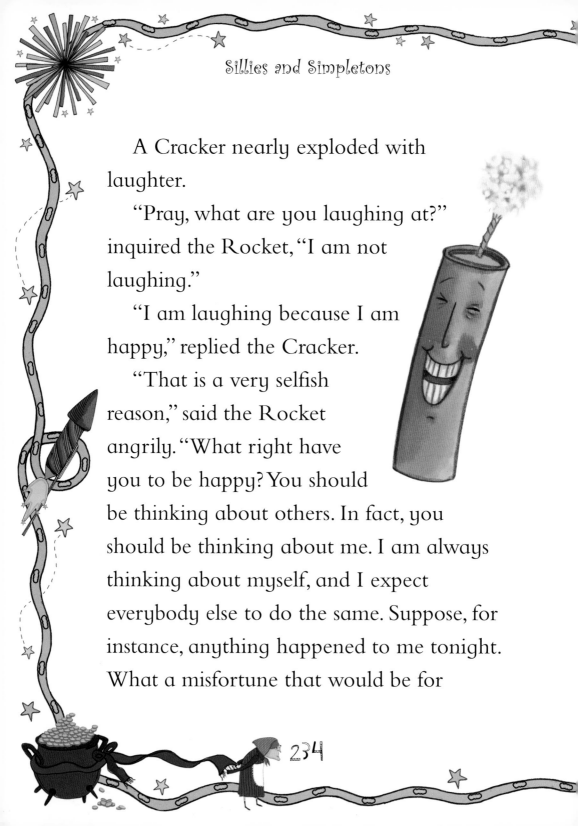

A Cracker nearly exploded with laughter.

"Pray, what are you laughing at?" inquired the Rocket, "I am not laughing."

"I am laughing because I am happy," replied the Cracker.

"That is a very selfish reason," said the Rocket angrily. "What right have you to be happy? You should be thinking about others. In fact, you should be thinking about me. I am always thinking about myself, and I expect everybody else to do the same. Suppose, for instance, anything happened to me tonight. What a misfortune that would be for everyone! The Prince and Princess would never be happy again—their whole married life would be spoiled, and as for the King, I know he would not get over it. Really, when I begin to think about the importance of my position, I am almost moved to tears."

"If you want to give pleasure to others," cried the Roman Candle, "you had better keep yourself dry."

"Certainly," exclaimed the Bengal Light. "That is only common sense."

"Common sense, indeed!" said the Rocket indignantly. "You forget that I am very uncommon, and very remarkable. Besides, none of you have any hearts. Here you are laughing and making merry just as if the Prince and Princess had not just been married."

"Well, really," exclaimed a small Fire-balloon, "why not? It is a most joyful occasion, and when I soar up into the air I intend to tell the stars all about it. You will see them twinkle when I talk to them about the pretty bride."

"Ah! What a simple view of life!" said the Rocket. "But it is only what I expected. There is nothing in you—you are hollow and empty. Why, perhaps the Prince and Princess may go to live in a country where there is a deep river, and perhaps they may have only one son—a little fair-haired boy with violet eyes like the Prince himself, and perhaps some day he may go out to walk with his nurse, and perhaps the nurse may go to sleep under a great elder tree, and perhaps the little boy may fall into the deep river and be drowned. What a terrible misfortune! Poor people, to lose their only son! It is really too dreadful! I shall never get over it."

"But they have not lost their only son," said the Roman Candle. "No misfortune has happened to them at all."

"I never said that they had," replied the Rocket. "I said that they might. If they had lost their only son there would be no use in saying anything more about the matter. I hate people who cry over spilled milk. But when I think that they might lose their only son, I certainly am very much affected."

"You certainly are!" cried the Bengal Light. "In fact, you are the most affected person I ever met."

"You are the rudest person I ever met," said the Rocket, quite offended, "and you cannot understand my friendship for the Prince."

"You had really better keep yourself dry," said the Fire-balloon. "That is the important thing."

"Very important for you, I have no doubt," answered the Rocket, "but I shall weep if I choose." And he actually burst into real tears, which flowed down his stick like raindrops. They nearly drowned two little beetles who were just thinking of setting up house together, and were looking for a nice dry spot to live in.

Then the moon rose like a silver shield and the stars began to shine, and a sound of music came from the palace.

The Prince and Princess were leading the dance. They danced so beautifully that the tall white lilies peeped in at the window and watched them, and the great red poppies nodded their heads and beat time.

Then ten o'clock struck, and then eleven, and then twelve, and at the last stroke of midnight everyone came out on the terrace.

"Let the fireworks begin," said the King, and the Royal Officer of Fireworks made a low bow, and marched down to the end of the garden. He had six attendants with him, each of whom carried a lighted torch at the end of a long pole.

It was certainly a magnificent display. *Whizz! Whizz!* went the Catharine Wheel, as she spun round and round. *Boom! Boom!* went the Roman Candle. Then the Squibs danced all over the place, and the Bengal Lights made everything look scarlet. "Goodbye," cried the Fire-balloon, as he soared away dropping tiny blue sparks. *Bang! Bang!* answered the Crackers, who were enjoying themselves immensely. Every one was a great success, except the Remarkable Rocket. He was so damp with crying that he could not go off at all. The best thing in him was the gunpowder, and that was so wet with tears that it was of no use. All his poor relations, to whom he would never speak, except with a sneer, shot up into the sky like wonderful golden flowers with blossoms of fire.

"Huzza! Huzza!" cried the court, and the little Princess laughed with pleasure.

"I suppose they are reserving me for some grand occasion," said the Rocket, "no doubt that is what it means," and he looked more haughty than ever as the ball finished.

The next day the workmen came to put everything tidy. "This is evidently a welcome party sent for me," said the Rocket to himself, "I will receive them with suitable dignity." So he put his nose in the air, and began to frown severely as if he were thinking about some very important subject. But they took no notice of him at all till they were just going away. Then one of them caught sight of him. "Hallo!" he cried, "What a bad rocket!" and he threw him over the wall into the ditch.

"*Bad* Rocket? *Bad* Rocket?" said the Rocket as he whirled through the air. "Impossible! *Grand* Rocket, that is what the man said. *Bad* and *grand* sound very much the same, indeed they often are the same," and he fell into the mud. "It is not comfortable here," he remarked, "but no doubt it is some fashionable health spa, and they have sent me to improve my health. My nerves are certainly very much shattered, and I need rest."

After some time a large white duck swam by. She had yellow legs and webbed feet, and was considered a great beauty on account of her waddle.

"Quack, quack, quack," she said. "What a curious shape you are! Were you born like that, or is it the result of an accident?"

"It is quite evident that you have always lived in the country," answered the Rocket, "otherwise you would know who I am. However, I will excuse your ignorance. It would be unfair to expect other people to be as remarkable as oneself. You will no doubt be surprised to hear that I can fly up into the sky, and come down in a shower of golden rain."

"I don't think much of that," said the Duck, "as I cannot see what use it is to anyone. Now, if you could plow the fields like the ox, or draw a cart like the horse, or look after the sheep like the collie dog, that would be something."

"My good creature," cried the Rocket in a very haughty tone of voice, "a person of my position is never useful. We have certain beauties, and that is more than enough."

"Well, well," said the Duck, who was of a very peaceable disposition, and never quarreled with anyone, "everybody has different tastes. I hope, at any rate, that you are going to live here."

"Oh! Dear no," cried the Rocket. "I am merely a visitor, a distinguished visitor. The fact is that I find this place rather dull. I shall probably go back to court, for I know that I am destined to make a sensation in the world. I am made to be famous," said the Rocket, "and so are all my relations, even the humblest of them. Whenever we appear we excite great attention. I have not actually appeared myself, but when I do so it will be a magnificent sight."

"Ah! The higher things of life, how fine they are!" said the Duck. "And that reminds me how hungry I feel." And she swam away down the stream, saying, "Quack, quack, quack."

"Come back! Come back!" screamed the Rocket. "I have a great deal to say to you," but the Duck paid no attention to him.

He sank a little deeper still into the mud, when suddenly two little boys in white smocks came running down the bank with a kettle and a bundle of sticks for making a fire. "Hello!" cried one of the boys. "Look at this old stick! I wonder how it came here," and he picked the rocket out of the ditch.

"*Old* stick!" said the Rocket indignantly. "Impossible! *Gold* stick, that is what he said. *Gold* stick is very complimentary."

"Let us put it into the fire!" said the other boy. "It will help to boil the kettle."

So they piled the sticks together, put the Rocket on top, and lit the fire.

"This is magnificent," cried the Rocket, "they are going to let me off in broad daylight, so that everyone can see me."

"We will go to sleep now," the boys said, "and when we wake up the kettle will be boiled." So they lay down on the grass and shut their eyes.

The Rocket was very damp, so he took a long time to burn. At last, however, the fire caught him.

"Now I am going off!" he cried, and he made himself very stiff and straight. "I know I shall go much higher than the stars, much higher than the moon, much higher than the sun. In fact, I shall go so high that—"

Fizz! Fizz! Fizz! and he went straight up into the air.

"Delightful!" he cried. "I shall go on like this forever. What a success I am!"

But nobody saw him.

Then he began to feel a curious tingling sensation all over him.

"Now I am going to explode," he cried. "I shall set the whole world on fire and make such a noise that nobody will talk about anything else for a year."

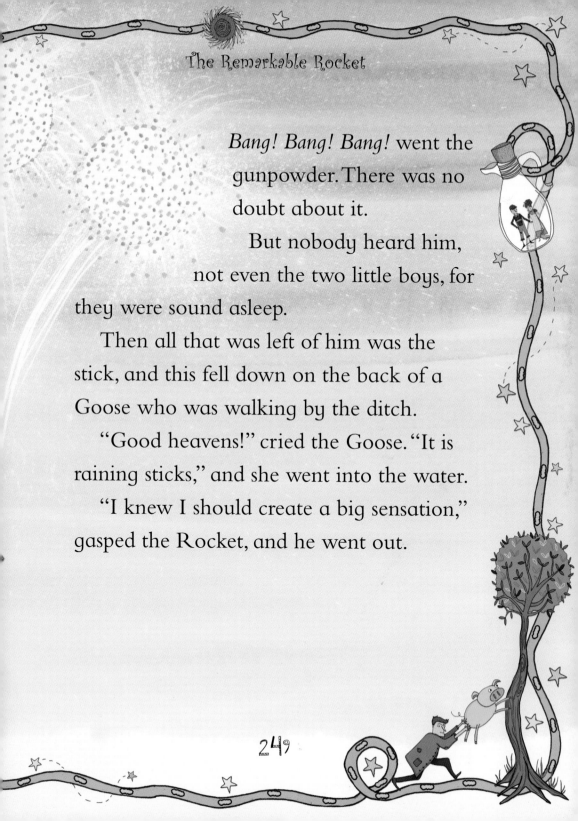

Bang! Bang! Bang! went the gunpowder. There was no doubt about it.

But nobody heard him, not even the two little boys, for they were sound asleep.

Then all that was left of him was the stick, and this fell down on the back of a Goose who was walking by the ditch.

"Good heavens!" cried the Goose. "It is raining sticks," and she went into the water.

"I knew I should create a big sensation," gasped the Rocket, and he went out.

The King's New Turban

By Sheykh-Zada, translated by E. J. W. Gibb

Once upon a time, very long ago, there was a great king. One day a man came before him and said, "My King, I shall weave a turban and only one who is intelligent shall be able to see it, while anyone foolish will not."

The King marveled and ordered that the

weaver should weave that turban. He ordered that the weaver be given whatever materials he required and as much money as was necessary to cover all the expenses. The weaver locked himself away in a private room and got going without further delay.

The King waited for days… and for weeks… and months… growing ever more impatient and excited to see his magical, mysterious turban.

At last the day came when the weaver once more came to see the King, very carefully carrying a flat, thin paper parcel. "O King," he announced, bowing very low, "your wish is my command. Here is your precious, priceless turban."

251

His eyes gleaming with excitement, the King tore off the paper and saw that there was… nothing in the weaver's outstretched, flat palms. All the viziers and nobles who stood there looked at the weaver's hands and, instead of seeing a folded length of gloriously woven material ready to be wound into a turban, saw *nothing*.

The King's face fell and he said in his heart, 'Oh my goodness! I must be a fool!' He was absolutely crushed!

Then straight away he thought, 'But I have no choice—I will have to pretend! I will have to say it is a wonderful turban and admire it, or else I will be put to shame before everybody. All my servants and subjects will know that I have been shown to be an idiot!' So he forced himself to smile and say, "Oh it is a wonderful turban, I like it very much."

Then the weaver said, "O King, let them bring a cap that I may wind the turban for you." They

253

brought a cap and put it on the King's head, and the weaver moved his hands as though he wound the turban.

All the nobles who were standing there said, "Blessed be it! O King, how fair, how beautiful a turban!" and they applauded it with great enthusiasm.

The King swallowed hard. He summoned his two closest advisors to accompany him into a private room and locked the door. Then he span round and hissed, "O viziers, I must be the world's greatest fool, for I cannot see the turban!"

The viziers looked at each other, then back at the king, and admitted, "O King, we, too, can't see it!"

Then all three rushed to unlock the door,

so they could catch the weaver and have him thrown into the deepest, darkest dungeon. But of course—the weaver was gone, out of the palace, off into the narrow streets of the city, vanished without a trace —taking all the money the King had paid along with him.

The Hedley Kow

By Joseph Jacobs

There was once an old woman who earned a poor living by running errands and suchlike for the farmers' wives round about the village where she lived. It wasn't much she earned by it, but with a plate of meat at one house and a cup of tea at another, she managed to get by somehow, and always looked as cheerful as if she hadn't a want in the world.

Well, one summer evening as the old woman was trotting away homeward, she came upon a big, black pot lying at the side of the road.

"Now that," said she, stopping to look at it, "would be just the very thing for me if I had anything to put into it! But who could have left it here?" and she looked round about, as if the person it belonged to must be not far off. But she could see no one.

"Maybe it'll have a hole in it," she said thoughtfully. "Ay, that'll be why they've left it lying. But then it'd do fine to put a flower in for the window, I'm thinking I'll just take it home anyways." And she bent her stiff old back, and lifted the lid to look inside.

"Mercy me!" she cried, and jumped

back to the other side of the road. "If it isn't full to the brim o' gold pieces!"

For a while she could do nothing but walk round and round her treasure, admiring the yellow gold and wondering at her good luck, and saying to herself about every two minutes, "Well, I do be feeling rich and grand!" But presently she began to think how she could best take it home with her. She couldn't see any other way than by fastening one end of her shawl to it and dragging it after her along the road.

"It'll certainly be dark soon," she said to herself, "and folk'll not see what I'm bringing home with me, and so I'll have all the night to myself to think what I'll do with it. I could buy a grand house and all, and live like the Queen herself, and not do a stroke of work all day, but just sit by the fire with a cup of tea. Or maybe I'll give it to the priest to keep for me, and get a piece whenever I want. Or maybe I'll just bury it in a hole at the bottom of the garden, and put one gold piece on the chimney, between the china teapot and the spoons—for ornament like. Ah! I feel so grand, I don't know myself!"

By this time, being already rather tired with dragging such a heavy weight after her, the old woman stopped to rest for a minute, turning to make sure that her treasure was safe.

But when she looked back at it, it wasn't a pot of gold at all, but a great lump of shining silver!

She stared at it, and rubbed her eyes and stared at it again, but she couldn't make it look like anything but a great lump of silver. "I'd have sworn it was a pot of gold," she said at last, "but I reckon I must have been dreaming. Ay, now, that's a change for the better. It'll be far less trouble to look after, and not so easily stolen. Those gold pieces would have been a lot of bother to keep safe anyway. Ay, I'm well quit of them, and with my bonny lump I'm as rich as rich!"

She set off homeward again, cheerfully planning all the grand things she was going to do with her money. It wasn't very long, however, before she got tired again and so she stopped once more to rest for a minute or two.

Again she turned to look at her treasure, and as soon as she set eyes on it she cried out in astonishment, "Oh, my!" said she, "now it's a lump o' iron! Well, that beats all,

263

and it's just real convenient! I can sell it as easy as easy, and get a lot o' penny pieces for it. Ay, an' it's much handier than a lot o' yer gold and silver—those would have kept me from sleeping at night thinking the neighbors were robbing me! An' it's a real good thing to have by you in a house. You never can tell what you mightn't use it for—an' it'll sell, ay, for a real lot. Rich? I'll be just rolling!"

And on she trotted again, chuckling to herself on her good luck, till presently she glanced over her shoulder, "Just to make sure it was there still," she said to herself.

"Eh, my!" she cried as soon as she saw it. "If it hasn't gone and turned itself into a great stone this time! Now, how could it have known that I was just terrible wanting something to hold my door open with? Ay, if that isn't a good change! It's a fine thing to have such good luck."

All in a hurry to see how the stone would look in its corner by her door, she trotted off down the hill, and stopped beside her own little gate.

When she had unlatched it, she turned to unfasten her shawl from the stone, which this time seemed to lie unchanged and peaceably on the path beside her. There was still plenty of light, and she could see the stone quite plainly as she bent her stiff back over it to untie the shawl end.

Then, all of a sudden, it seemed to give a jump and a squeal, and grew in a moment

as big as a great horse. Then it threw
down four lanky legs and shook
out two long ears,
flourished a tail, and
went off kicking its
feet into the air and
laughing like a
naughty, mocking boy.

The old woman stared
after it, till it was fairly out
of sight.

"*Well!*" she said at last, "I
do be the luckiest body hereabouts!
I'd heard of that magical Hedley
Kow that plays tricks on unsuspecting
folk, but I never dreamed I would see
it with my own eyes, all to myself!

I can tell you, I do feel
that *grand*!"
And she went into her cottage,
and sat down by the fire
to think over her
good luck.

The Darning Needle

By Hans Christian Andersen

There was once a Darning Needle who thought herself so fine, she imagined she was an embroidering needle. "Take care, and mind you hold me tight!" she said to the Fingers that took her out. "Don't let me fall! If I fall on the ground I shall certainly never be found again, for I am so fine!"

"That's as it may be," said the Fingers, and they grasped her round the body.

"See, I'm coming with a train!" said the Darning Needle, and she drew a long thread after her.

The Fingers pointed the needle just at the cook's slipper, in which the leather had burst and was to be sewn together.

"That's common work," said the Darning Needle. "I shall never get through. I'm far too fine. I'm breaking! I'm breaking!" And she really broke. "Did I not say so?" said the Darning Needle.

"Now this needle's quite useless," said the Fingers, but they were obliged to hold her all the same, for the cook dropped some sealing wax upon the needle to stick her back together again, and pinned the ends of her neck scarf together with it in front.

"So, now I'm a brooch!" said the Darning Needle. "I knew very well that I should become important!" And she laughed quietly to herself—of course one can never see when a Darning Needle laughs. There she sat, as proud as if she were in a state coach, and looked all about her. In fact, the Darning Needle drew herself up so proudly that she fell out of the neck scarf right into the sink, which the cook was rinsing out.

"Now I'm going on a journey," said the Darning Needle. "If I only don't get lost!"

But of course, she washed down the pipe and out into the drain and really was lost.

"I'm too fine for this world," she observed, as she lay in the gutter. "But I know who I am, and there's always something in that!"

So the Darning Needle kept her proud behavior, and did not lose her good humor. Things of many kinds swam over her—chips and straws and pieces of old newspapers.

"Only look how they sail!" said the Darning Needle. "They don't know what is under them! I'm here, I remain firmly here. See, there goes a chip thinking of nothing in the world but of himself—of a chip! There's a straw going by now. How he turns! How he twirls about! Don't think only of yourself, you might easily run up against a stone. There swims a bit of newspaper. What's written upon it has long been forgotten, and yet it gives itself airs. I sit quietly and patiently here. I know who I am, and I shall remain what I am."

One day something lay close beside her that glittered splendidly. The Darning Needle believed that it was a diamond, but it was a bit of broken bottle, and because it shone, the Darning Needle spoke to it, introducing herself as a brooch. "I suppose you are a diamond?" she observed.

"Why, yes, something of that kind."

Each believed the other to be a very valuable thing, and they began speaking about the world and how important they were in it.

"And now we sit here and glitter!" said the Bit of Bottle. But at that very moment more water came into the gutter and the Bit of Bottle was carried away.

"So he has gone," observed the Darning Needle. "I remain here. I am too fine." And proudly she sat there, and had many great thoughts. "I could almost believe I had been born of a sunbeam, I'm so fine! It really appears as if the sunbeams were always seeking for me under the water."

One day a couple of boys were playing in the gutter, where they sometimes found old nails, pennies, and similar treasures. It was dirty work, but they took delight in it.

"Oh!" cried one, who had pricked himself with the Darning Needle. "There's a fellow for you!"

"I'm not a fellow, I'm a young lady!" said the Darning Needle.

But nobody listened to her. The sealing wax had come off and she had turned black, but black makes one look slender, and she thought herself finer than ever.

"Here comes an eggshell sailing along!" said the boys, and they stuck the Darning

Needle fast in the eggshell.

"White walls, and black myself! That looks well," remarked the Darning Needle. "Now one can see me. I only hope I shall not be seasick!" But she was not seasick at all. "The finer one is, the more one can bear," she remarked.

Crack! went the eggshell, as a bicycle rode over her.

"Good heavens, how it crushes one!" said the Darning Needle. "I'm getting seasick now—I'm quite sick."

But she was not really sick, though the bicycle went over her—she lay there at full length, and there she may still lie.

Day-Dreaming

By Joseph Jacobs

Now there was once a man of Baghdad who had seven sons, and when he died he left to each of them one hundred dirhems.

His fifth son, called Alnaschar the Babbler, spent all this money on a precious vase, and he put it in a big tray from which to show and sell it. He sat down on a raised bench at the foot of a wall, against which he leaned back, placing the tray on the ground in front of him.

Day-Dreaming

As he sat he began day-dreaming, and said to himself, "I have spent a hundred dirhems on this vase. Now I will surely sell it for two hundred, and with that I will buy more vases and sell them for four hundred, and I will not cease to buy and sell till I become master of much wealth. With this I will buy all kinds of luxuries and jewels

and perfumes, and make great profit on
them till, God willing, I will have a hundred
thousand dinars or two million dirhems.
Then I will buy a handsome house,
together with servants and horses and
trappings of gold, and I will eat and drink
and be merry."

This he said looking at the tray before
him with a vase worth a hundred dirhems.

Then he continued, "When I have
amassed a hundred thousand dinars I will
demand the hand of the Vizier's daughter in
marriage, for I hear that she is perfect in
beauty. When I return home, I will hire ten
little servants, and clothes for myself such as
those worn by kings and sultans, and get a
saddle of gold set thick with precious jewels.

Then I will mount my horse and parade the city, with servants before and behind me, while the people will salute me and call down blessings upon me.

"Then I will go to the Vizier, the girl's father, with servants behind and before me, as well as on either hand. When the Vizier sees me, he will rise and seat me in his own place, while he himself sits down below me, because I am his son-in-law. I will have with me two servants with purses, and I will offer him a present of a thousand dinars so that he may recognize my nobility, generosity, and greatness of mind, and for every ten words he will say to me, I will answer him only two.

"Then I will return to my house. If

anyone comes to see me, I will give him a present of money and dress him in a beautiful robe of honor. If he brings me a present, I will return it to him and will not accept it so that they may know how great of soul I am.

"Then I will command them to bring the Vizier's daughter to me in a grand procession, and I will get my house ready to receive her. When the time of the unveiling of the bride comes, I will put on my richest clothes and sit down on a couch of silk, leaning on a cushion, and looking straight ahead to show how important I am. My bride shall stand before me like the full moon, in her robes and jewels. Out of pride, I will not look at her till all who are present

278

say to me, 'O my lord, your wife stands before you, look upon her.' And they will kiss the earth before me many times. So I will lift my eyes and glance at her once, then bend down my head again.

"Then they will carry her to the bride chamber, and meanwhile I will rise and change my clothes for a richer suit. When they bring in the bride for the second time, I will not look at her till they have begged me to do so several times. Then I will glance at her and bow down my head. Then I will order one of my servants to fetch a purse, and, giving it to the bridesmaids, command them to lead her to the bride chamber.

"When they leave me alone with the bride, I will not look at her or speak to her, but will sit by her without looking, so that she may say I am a good man with a pure soul. Her mother will come to me and kiss my head and hands, and say to me, 'O my lord, look on your bride, for she longs for your favor.'

"Then she will fetch a cup of wine, and her daughter will take it and come to me, but I will leave her standing while I lay back upon a cushion. I will not look at her, so that she will think me to be a sultan of great dignity. She will say to me, 'O my lord, for God's sake, do not refuse to take this cup, for indeed I am yours.' But I will not speak to her, and she will press me, saying, 'Please, drink,' and put it to my lips. Then I will shake my fist and push her away with my foot, so…"

So saying, Alnaschar gave a kick with his foot and knocked over the vase, which fell over and was broken to bits.

The Simpleton

By Andrew Lang

Once upon a time there lived a man who was as rich as he could be, but as no happiness in this world is ever quite complete, he had an only son who was such a simpleton that he could barely add two and two together. At last his father determined to put up with his stupidity no longer and, giving him a purse full of gold, sent him to seek his fortune in foreign lands, telling him to be mindful of the saying:

"How much a fool that's sent to roam
Excels a fool that stays at home."

Moscione, for this was the youth's name,
mounted a horse and set out for Venice,
hoping to find a ship there that would take
him to Cairo. After he had ridden for some
time he saw a man standing at the foot of a
poplar tree, and said to him, "What's your
name, my friend? Where do you come from,
and what can you do?"

The man replied, "My name is Quick-
as-Thought and I come from Fleet-town. I
can run like lightning."

"I should like to see you," returned
Moscione.

"Just wait a minute, then," said

Quick-as-Thought, "and I will soon show you that I am speaking the truth."

The words were hardly out of his mouth when a young doe ran right across the field they were standing in.

Quick-as-Thought let her run on a short distance, in order to give her a start, and then pursued her so quickly and so lightly that you could not have tracked his footsteps if the field had been strewn with flour. In a few springs he had overtaken the doe. He had so impressed Moscione with his fleetness of foot that he begged Quick-as-Thought to go with him, promising at the same time to reward him handsomely.

Quick-as-Thought agreed to his proposal, and they continued on their journey together. They had hardly gone a mile when they met a young man, and Moscione stopped and asked him, "What's your name, my friend? Where do you come from, and what can you do?"

The man answered promptly, "I am called Hare's-Ear and I come from Curiosity Valley. If I lay my ear on the ground, without moving from the spot, I can hear everything that goes on in the world—the plots and gossip of court and cottage, and all the plans of mice and men."

"If that's the case," replied Moscione, "tell me what's going on in my own home at present."

The youth laid his ear to the ground and at once reported, "An old man is saying to his wife, 'Heaven be praised that we have got rid of Moscione, for perhaps, when he has been out in the world a little, he may gain some common sense, and return home less of a fool than when he set out.'"

"Enough, enough," cried Moscione. "You speak the truth, and I believe you. Come with us and your fortune's made."

The young man consented, and after they had gone about ten miles, they met a third man, to whom Moscione said, "What's your name, my brave fellow? Where were you born, and what can you do?"

The man replied, "I am called Hit-the-Point, I come from the city of Perfect-aim, and I draw my bow so exactly that I can shoot a pea off a stone."

"I should like to see you do it, if you've no objection," said Moscione.

The man at once placed a pea on a stone, and, drawing his bow, he shot it through the middle with the greatest possible ease.

When Moscione saw that the man had spoken the truth, he immediately asked

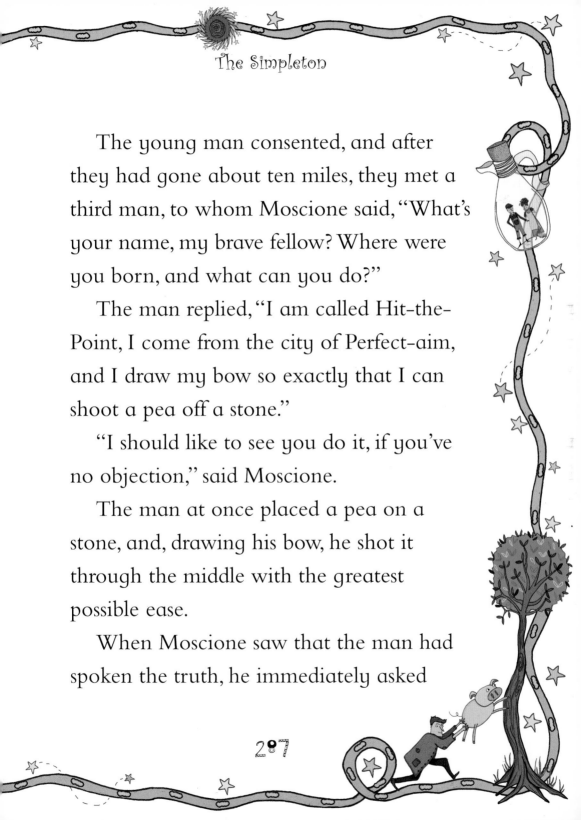

Hit-the-Point to join his party.

After they had all traveled together for some days, they came upon a number of people who were digging a trench in the blazing sun. Moscione felt so sorry for them that he said, "My dear friends, how can you stand working so hard in heat that would cook an egg in a minute?"

But one of the workmen answered, "We are as fresh as daisies, for we have a young man among us who blows on our backs like the west wind."

"Let me see him," said Moscione.

The youth was called, and Moscione asked him, "What's your name? Where do you come from, and what can you do?"

He answered, "I am called Blow-Blast. I

come from Wind-town, and with my mouth I can make any winds you please. If you wish a west wind I can raise it for you in a second, but if you prefer a north wind I can blow these houses down before your eyes."

"Seeing is believing," returned the cautious Moscione.

Blow-Blast at once began to convince him of the truth of his statement. First he blew so softly that it seemed like the gentle breeze at evening, and then he turned round and raised such a mighty storm that he blew down a whole row of oak trees.

When Moscione saw this he was delighted, and begged Blow-Blast to join his company. As they went on their way they met another man, whom Moscione

289

addressed as usual, "What's your name? Where do you come from, and what can you do?"

"I am called Strong-Back. I come from Power-borough. I possess such strength that I can take a mountain on my back and it seems a feather to me," the man replied.

"If that's the case," said Moscione, "I should like some proof of your strength."

Then Strong-Back loaded himself with great boulders and tree trunks, so that a hundred wagons could not have taken away all that he carried on his back.

When Moscione saw this he persuaded Strong-Back to join his troop, and they all continued on their journey till they came to a country called Flower Vale.

Here there reigned a king whose only daughter could run as quickly as the wind, and so lightly that she could run over a field of young oats without bending a single blade. The King had given out a proclamation that anyone who could beat the Princess in a race should have her for a wife, but that all who failed should lose their head.

As soon as Moscione heard of the royal proclamation, he hurried to see the King and challenged the Princess to race with him. But on the morning appointed for the trial he sent word to the King that he was not feeling well, and that as he could not run himself he would supply someone to take his place.

"It's just the same to me," said Canetella, the Princess. "Let anyone come forward that likes. I am quite prepared to meet him."

At the time appointed for the race the whole place was crowded with lots of people anxious to see the contest. Punctual to the moment, Quick-as-Thought and Canetella who was dressed in a short skirt and very light shoes appeared at the starting point.

Then a silver trumpet sounded. The two rivals started on their race, looking for all the world like a greyhound chasing a hare.

But Quick-as-Thought, true to his name, outran the Princess, and when the goal was reached, the people all clapped their hands and shouted, "Long live the stranger!"

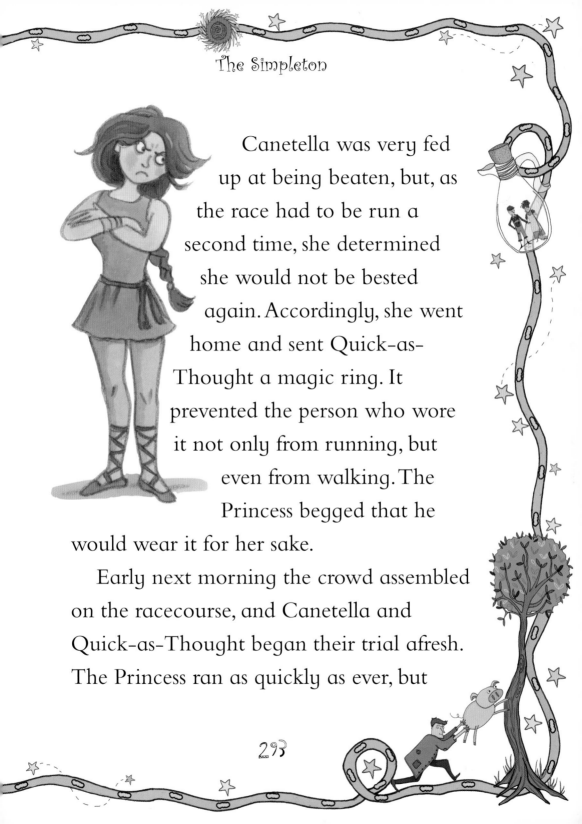

Canetella was very fed up at being beaten, but, as the race had to be run a second time, she determined she would not be bested again. Accordingly, she went home and sent Quick-as-Thought a magic ring. It prevented the person who wore it not only from running, but even from walking. The Princess begged that he would wear it for her sake.

Early next morning the crowd assembled on the racecourse, and Canetella and Quick-as-Thought began their trial afresh. The Princess ran as quickly as ever, but poor Quick-as-Thought was like an overloaded donkey, and could not go a step.

Hit-the-Point had heard all about the Princess's trick from Hare's-Ear. When he saw the danger his friend was in, he seized his bow and arrow and, with perfect aim, shot the stone out of the ring that Quick-as-Thought was wearing. In a moment the youth's legs became free again, and in five bounds he had overtaken Canetella and won the race.

The King was much disgusted when he saw that he must acknowledge Moscione as his future son-in-law, and summoned the wise men of his court to ask if there was no way out of the difficulty.

The council at once decided that

Canetella was far too dainty a girl to become the wife of such a traveling tinker. They advised the King to offer Moscione a present of gold, which no doubt a beggar like him would prefer to all the wives in the world.

The King was delighted at this suggestion. He called Moscione before him and asked him what sum of money he would take instead of his promised bride.

Moscione first consulted with his friends, and then answered, "I demand as much gold and precious stones as my followers can carry away."

The King thought he was being let off very easily. He produced coffers of gold, sacks of silver, and chests of precious stones, but the more Strong-Back was loaded with the treasure the straighter he stood.

At last the treasury was quite exhausted. The King had to send his courtiers to his subjects to collect all the gold and silver they possessed. But nothing was of any avail, and Strong-Back only asked for more.

When the King's councilors saw the unexpected result of their advice, they said it would be more than foolish to let some strolling thieves take so much treasure out of the country, and urged the King to send soldiers after them.

So the King sent a body of armed men on foot and horse to take back the treasure Strong-Back was carrying away with him.

But Hare's-Ear had heard what the

councilors had advised the King and told his companions just as the dust of their pursuers was visible on the horizon.

No sooner had Blow-Blast taken in their danger than he raised such a mighty wind that all the King's army was blown down like ninepins. As they were unable to get up again, Moscione and his companions went on their way without further ado.

As soon as they reached his home, Moscione divided his spoil with his companions. He stayed with his father, who was forced to admit at last that his son was not such a fool as he looked.

A Visitor from Paradise

By Joseph Jacobs

There was once a woman, good but simple, whose first husband died, so she married again. One day, when her second husband was out working in the fields, a weary tramp came trudging by her door and asked for a drink of water. When she handed it to him, and being rather a gossip, she asked where he came from.

"From Paris," said the man.

The woman was a little bit deaf and
thought the man said "from paradise."
"From paradise! Did you meet my poor
dear husband there, Lord rest his soul?"

"What was his name?" asked the man.

"Why, John Goody, of course," said the
woman. "Did you know him in paradise?"

"What, John Goody!" said the man.
"Him and me was as thick as thieves."

"Does he want for anything?" said the
woman. "I suppose up in paradise you get
all you want."

"All we want? Why, look at me," said the
man pointing to his rags and tatters. "They
treat some of us right shabby up there."

"Dear me, that's bad. Are you likely to go back?"

"Go back to paradise, marm? I should say. We have to be in every night at ten."

"Well, perhaps you wouldn't mind taking back some things for my poor old John," said the woman.

"Of course, madam. Delighted to help my old chum John."

So the woman went indoors and got a big pile of clothes, a long pipe, three bottles of beer, and a beer jug, and gave them to the man. "But," he said, "please, I can't carry all these by my own self. Haven't you got a horse or a donkey that I can take along with me to carry them? I'll bring him back tomorrow."

Then the woman said, "There's our old Dobbin in the stable. I can't lend you mare Juniper 'cause my husband's plowing with her just now."

"Ah, well, Dobbin'll do as it's only until tomorrow."

The woman got out Dobbin and saddled him, and the man took the clothes, pipe, and beer, then rode off with them.

Shortly afterward the woman's husband came

home and said, "What's become of Dobbin?
He's not in the stable."

So his wife told him all that had
happened. He said, "I don't like that. How
do we know that he is going to paradise?
How do we know that he'll bring Dobbin
back tomorrow? I'll saddle Juniper and get
our things back. Which way did he go?"

So her husband saddled Juniper and rode
after the man, who saw him coming afar
off and guessed what had happened. So he
got off from Dobbin and drove him into a
clump of trees near the roadside, and then
went and laid down on his back and looked
up to the sky. When the farmer came up to
him, he got down from Juniper and said,
"What are you doing there?"

"Oh, such a funny thing," said the man. "A fellow came along here on a horse with some clothes and things, and when he got to the top of the hill here he simply gave a shout and the horse went right up into the sky. I was watching him just now when you came up."

"Oh, it's all right then," said the farmer. "He's gone to paradise, sure enough," and went back to his wife.

Next day they waited, and they waited for the man to bring back Dobbin, but he didn't come that day nor the next day, nor the next.

And they are still waiting.

The Blind Men and the Elephant

By James Baldwin

There were once six blind men who stood by the roadside every day, and scraped out a living by begging from the people who passed. They knew that all sorts of sights passed them by, for they heard all the talk of the travelers who went up and down the road. But they had never seen anything, for being blind, how could they?

It so happened one morning that an

elephant was driven down the road where they stood. When they were told that such a great beast was before them, they asked the driver to let him stop so that they might see him.

Of course they could not see him with their eyes, but they thought that by touching him they could learn just what kind of animal he was.

The first one happened to put his hand on the elephant's side. "Well, well!" he said. "Now I know all about this beast. He is exactly like a wall."

The second felt only of the elephant's tusk. "My brother," he said, "you are mistaken. He is not at all like a wall. He is

round and smooth and
sharp. He is more like a
spear than anything else."

The third happened to take hold of the elephant's trunk. "Both of you are wrong," he said. "Anybody who knows anything can see that this elephant is like a snake."

The fourth reached out his arms, and grasped one of the elephant's legs. "Oh, how blind you are!" he said. "It is very plain to me that he is round and tall like a tree."

The fifth chanced to take hold of the elephant's ear. "The blindest man ought to know that this beast is not like any of the things that you name," he said. "He is just like a huge fan."

The sixth was very blind indeed, and it was some time before he could find the elephant at all. At last he seized the animal's tail. "O foolish fellows!" he cried. "You surely have lost your senses. This elephant is not like a wall, or a spear, or a snake, or a tree, neither is he like a fan. But any man with a particle of sense can see that he is exactly like a rope."

Then the elephant moved on, and the six blind men sat by the roadside all day, and quarreled about it. Each believed that he knew just how the animal looked, and each called the others names because they did not agree with him.

People who have eyes sometimes act just as foolishly.

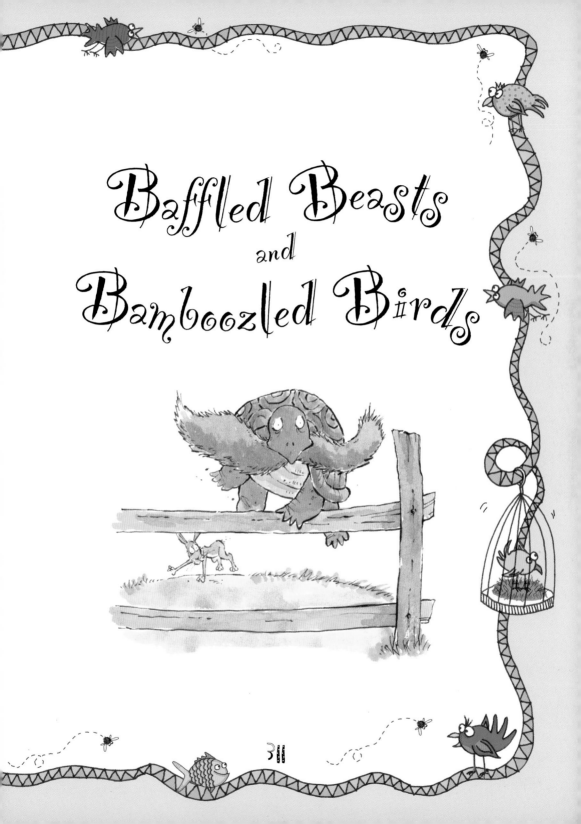

Baffled Beasts
and
Bamboozled Birds

The Open Road

An extract from *The Wind in the Willows*
by Kenneth Grahame

*The Mole has just moved into a new home at the riverbank
when he makes friends with the Water Rat, who introduces him
to the joy of messing around in boats…*

"Ratty," said Mole, "what I wanted to ask
you was, won't you take me to call on
Mr. Toad? I've heard so much about him,
and I would like to make his acquaintance."

"Why, certainly," said the good-natured

Rat, jumping to his feet. "Get the boat out, and we'll paddle up there at once. It's never the wrong time to call on Toad. Early or late, he's always the same fellow. Always good-tempered, always glad to see you, always sorry when you go!"

"He must be a very nice animal," observed the Mole, as he got into the boat and took the sculls, while the Rat settled himself comfortably in the stern.

"He is indeed the best of animals," replied Rat. "So simple, so good-natured, and so affectionate. Perhaps he's not very clever—we can't all be geniuses—and it may be that he is both boastful and conceited. But he has got some great qualities, has Toady."

Rounding a bend in the river, they came in sight of a handsome, dignified old house of mellowed red brick, with well-kept lawns reaching down to the water's edge.

"There's Toad Hall," said the Rat.

They glided up the creek, and the Mole slipped his sculls as they passed into the shadow of a large boathouse. Here they saw many handsome boats, but none in the water. The place had an unused and deserted air.

The Rat looked around him. "I understand," said he. "Boating is played out. He's tired of it and done with it. I wonder what new fad he has taken up now?"

They disembarked and strolled across the flower-decked lawns in search of Toad,

whom they presently
happened upon resting in
a wicker garden chair,
with a preoccupied
expression on his
face, and a large
map spread out
on his knees.

"Hooray!" he
cried, jumping up on
seeing them. "This is splendid!" He shook
the paws of both of them warmly, never
waiting for an introduction to the Mole. "I
need both of you—badly! You've got to
help me. It's most important!"

"It's about your rowing, I suppose," said
the Rat. "You're getting on fairly well,

though you splash a good bit still. With a great deal of patience, and any quantity of coaching, you may—"

"Oh, pooh! Boating!" interrupted the Toad, in great disgust. "Silly boyish amusement. I've given that up *long* ago. Waste of time, that's what it is. No, I've discovered the real thing. Come with me, and you shall see what you shall see!"

He led the way to the stable yard, the Rat following with a most mistrustful expression. There, drawn out of the coach house into the open, they saw a gypsy caravan, shining with newness, painted a canary-yellow picked out with green, and red wheels.

"There you are!" cried the Toad, puffing out his chest with pride. "There's real life for you, embodied in that little cart. The open road, the dusty highway, the heath, the common, the hedgerows, the rolling downs! Camps, villages, towns, cities! Here today, up and off to somewhere else tomorrow! Travel, change, interest, excitement! The whole world before you, and a horizon that's always changing! And mind— this is the very finest cart of its sort that was ever built, without any exception! Come inside and look at the arrangements. Planned 'em all myself, I did!"

The Mole was tremendously interested and excited, and followed the Toad eagerly up the steps and inside. The Rat only snorted and thrust his hands deep into his pockets, remaining where he was.

It was indeed very compact and comfortable. Little sleeping bunks, a little table that folded up against the wall, a cooking stove, lockers, bookshelves, a birdcage with a bird in it, and pots, pans, jugs, and kettles of every size and variety.

"All complete!" said the Toad triumphantly, pulling open a locker. "You see—biscuits, potted lobster, sardines— everything you can possibly want. Soda

water here, letter paper, bacon, jam, cards,
and dominoes there. You'll find," he
continued, as they descended the steps
again, "you'll find that nothing whatever
has been forgotten, when we make our start
this afternoon."

"I beg your pardon," said the Rat slowly,
as he chewed a straw, "but did I overhear
you say something about 'we,' and 'start,'
and 'this afternoon?'"

"Now, you dear good old Ratty," said
Toad, imploringly, "don't begin talking in
that stiff and sniffy sort of way, because you
know you really have *got* to come. I can't
possibly manage without you, so please
consider it settled, and don't argue—it's the
one thing I can't stand. You surely don't

mean to stick to your dull, fusty old river all your life, and just live in a hole in a bank, and *boat*? I want to show you the world, Ratty! I'm going to make an *animal* of you, my boy!"

"I don't care," said the Rat, doggedly. "I'm not coming, and that's flat. And I *am* going to stick to my old river, *and* live in a hole, *and* boat, as I've always done. And what's more, Mole's going to stick with me and do as I do, aren't you, Mole?"

"Of course I am," said the Mole, loyally. "I'll always stick to you, Rat, and what you say is to be—has got to be. All the same, it sounds as if it might have been—well, rather fun, you know!" he added, wistfully. Poor Mole! The Life Adventurous was so new a thing to him and so thrilling, and this fresh aspect of it was so tempting, and he had fallen in love at first sight with the canary-colored cart.

The Rat saw what was passing in his mind, and wavered. He hated disappointing people, and he was awfully fond of the Mole, and would do almost anything to oblige him. Toad was watching both of them closely.

"Come along in and have some lunch," he said, "and we'll talk it over. We needn't decide anything in a hurry. Of course, I don't really care. I only want to give pleasure to you fellows. 'Live for others!' That's my motto in life."

Needless to say, after lunch, the old gray

horse was caught and harnessed. Toad packed the lockers with necessaries, and hung feedbags, onions, bundles of hay, and baskets from the bottom of the cart.

They set off, all talking at once, each animal either trudging by the side of the cart or sitting on the shaft. It was a golden afternoon. The smell of the dust they kicked up was rich and satisfying. Out of orchards on either side of the road, birds called and whistled to them cheerily. Good-natured wayfarers called, "Good-day," or stopped to say nice things about their cart. Rabbits, sitting at their front doors in the hedgerows held up their forepaws and said, "Oh my! Oh my! Oh my!"

They had a pleasant ramble over grassy

downs and along narrow by-lanes, until at last they came out on the high road—and there disaster sprang out on them.

Far behind them they heard a faint warning hum, like the drone of a distant bee. Glancing back, they saw a small cloud of dust, with a dark center of energy, advancing on them at incredible speed, while from out of the dust a faint "Poop-poop!" wailed like an uneasy animal in pain. Hardly regarding it, they turned to resume their conversation, when in an instant (as it seemed) the peaceful scene was changed, with a blast of wind and a whirl of sound that made them jump for the nearest ditch.

It was on them! The "Poop-poop" rang

with a brazen shout in their ears. They had
a moment's glimpse of an interior of
glittering plate-glass and rich leather. The
magnificent motor car—immense, breath-
snatching, passionate—with its pilot tense
and hugging his wheel, possessed all earth
and air for the fraction of a second. Then
up flew an enveloping cloud of dust that
blinded and enwrapped them utterly, and
the car dwindled to a speck in the far
distance, changed back into a droning bee
once more.

The old gray horse, dreaming, as he
plodded along, of his quiet paddock, in a
new raw situation such as this simply
abandoned himself to his natural emotions.
Rearing, plunging, backing steadily, he

drove the cart backward toward the deep ditch at the side of the road. It wavered an instant—then there was a heart-rending *crash*—and the canary-colored cart, their pride and their joy, lay on its side in the ditch, an irredeemable wreck.

The Rat danced up and down in the road, simply transported with passion. "You villains!" he shouted after it, shaking both fists, "You scoundrels, you highwaymen, you—you—roadhogs! I'll have the law on you! I'll report you! I'll take you through all the courts!"

Meanwhile Toad sat straight down in the middle of the dusty road, his legs stretched out before him, and stared fixedly in the direction of the disappearing motor car. He

breathed short, his face wore a placid
satisfied expression, and at intervals
he murmured, "Poop-poop!"

The Mole was busy
trying to calm the horse,
which he succeeded in doing after a time.
Then he went to look at the cart on its side
in the ditch. It was indeed a sorry sight.

Panels and windows smashed, axles hopelessly bent, one wheel off, sardine tins scattered over the wide world, and the bird in the birdcage sobbing pitifully and calling to be let out.

The Rat came to help him, but their united efforts were not sufficient to right the cart. "Hi! Toad!" they cried. "Come and lend a hand, will you!"

The Toad never answered a word, or budged from his seat in the road, so they went to see what was the matter with him. They found him in a sort of a trance, a happy smile on his face, his eyes still fixed on the dusty wake of their destroyer. At intervals he was still heard to murmur, "Poop-poop!"

The Rat shook him by the shoulder. "Are you coming to help us, Toad?" he demanded sternly.

"Glorious, stirring sight!" murmured Toad, never offering to move. "The poetry of motion! The *real* way to travel! The *only* way to travel! Here today—in next week tomorrow! Villages skipped, towns and cities jumped—always somebody else's horizon! Oh bliss! Oh poop-poop! Oh my! Oh my!"

"Oh *stop* being an ass, Toad!" cried the Mole despairingly.

"And to think I never *knew*!" went on the Toad in a dreamy monotone. "All those wasted years that lie behind me, I never knew, never even *dreamed*! But *now*—but now that I know, now that I fully realize!

Oh what a flowery track lies spread before me, henceforth! What dust clouds shall spring up behind me as I speed on my reckless way! What carts I shall fling carelessly into the ditch in the wake of my magnificent onset! Horrid little carts— common carts—canary-colored carts!"

"What are we to do with him?" asked the Mole of the Water Rat.

"Nothing at all," replied the Rat firmly. "Because there is really nothing to be done. You see, I know him from of old. He is now possessed. He has got a new craze, and it always takes him that way in its first stage. He'll continue like that for days now, like an animal walking in a happy dream, quite useless for all practical purposes. Never mind him. Let's go and see what there is to be done about the cart."

A careful inspection showed them that, even if they succeeded in righting it by themselves, the cart would travel no longer. The axles were in a hopeless state, and the missing wheel was shattered into pieces.

The Rat knotted the horse's reins over his back and took him by the head, carrying the birdcage and its hysterical occupant in his other hand. "Come on!" he said grimly to the Mole. "It's five or six miles to the nearest town, and we shall just have to walk it. The sooner we make a start the better."

"But what about Toad?" asked the Mole anxiously. "We can't leave him here, in the middle of the road by himself, in the state he's in! It's not safe. Supposing another Thing were to come along?"

"Oh, *bother* Toad," said the Rat savagely, "I've done with him!"

They had not proceeded very far on their way, however, when there was a pattering of feet behind them. Toad caught them up and thrust a paw inside the elbow of each of them, still breathing short and staring into vacancy.

"Now, look here, Toad!" said the Rat sharply. "As soon as we get to the town, you'll have to go straight to the police station, and see if they know anything about that motor car, and lodge a complaint against it. Then you'll have to arrange for the cart to be fetched and mended. Meanwhile, the Mole and I will go to an inn and find rooms where we can stay till the cart's ready."

"Police station! Complaint!" murmured Toad dreamily. "Me *complain* of that beautiful vision! *Mend the cart!* I've done with carts. I never want to see or to hear of that cart again. Oh, Ratty! You can't think how obliged I am to you for coming on this trip! I wouldn't have gone without you, then I might never have seen that swan, that sunbeam, that thunderbolt! I might never have heard that entrancing sound, or smelled that bewitching smell! I owe it all to you, my best of friends!"

The Rat turned from him in despair. "He's quite hopeless" he said to the Mole. "When we get to the town we'll go to the railway station. With luck we may pick up a train that'll get us back to the riverbank tonight. *Never* let me go a-pleasuring with this provoking animal again!"

The following evening the Mole was sitting on the bank fishing, when the Rat came along to find him. "Heard the news?" he said. "Toad went up to town this morning. He has ordered a large and very expensive motor car."

Why the Bear is Stumpy-Tailed

By Sir George Webbe Dasent

One wintry day, when the fields were covered with snow and ice, and none of the animals could find food, Bruin the Bear met Reynard the Fox. To his surprise, Reynard was slinking along with a string of fish. How Bruin's stomach rumbled! Little did he know that Reynard had stolen them from the home of a farmer down the road. The slow old bear thought that the cunning fox must have come by them himself.

"Where ever did you find those?" asked the Bear, licking his lips.

"Oh my Lord Bruin, I've been out fishing and caught them," said Reynard the Fox.

So Bruin had a mind to learn to fish too. He begged Reynard tell him where to go and how to set about it.

"Oh, it will be an easy craft for you," answered the Fox. "All you've got to do is go out on the lake over the ice, cut a hole, and stick your tail down into it. Then go on holding it there as long as you can. Take no notice if your tail smarts a little—that's when the fish bite. Then, when you can wait no longer, pull your tail out as fast and as hard as you can."

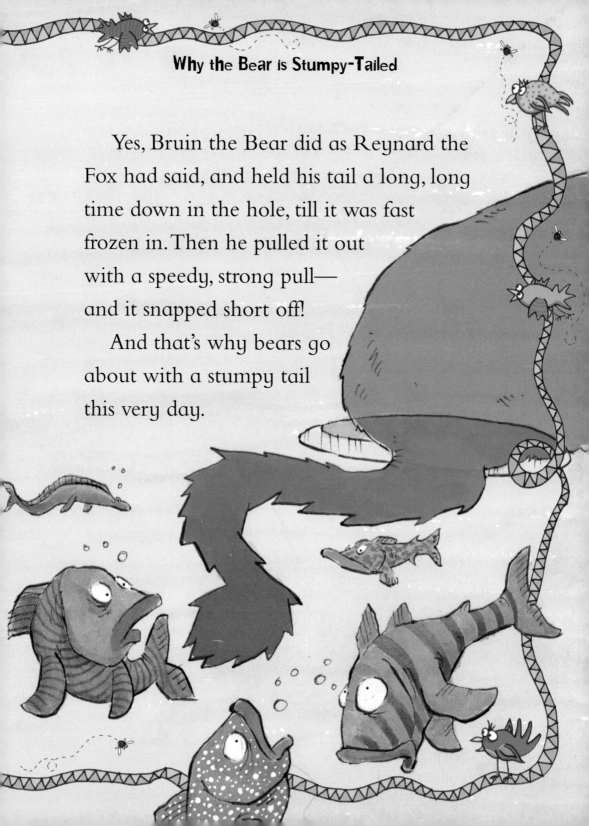

Why the Bear is Stumpy-Tailed

Yes, Bruin the Bear did as Reynard the
Fox had said, and held his tail a long, long
time down in the hole, till it was fast
frozen in. Then he pulled it out
with a speedy, strong pull—
and it snapped short off!

And that's why bears go
about with a stumpy tail
this very day.

The Rabbit's Bride

By the Brothers Grimm

There was once a woman who lived with her daughter in a beautiful cabbage garden. One day there came a rabbit and it ate up all the cabbages. So the woman said to her daughter, "Go into the garden, and drive out the rabbit."

"Shoo! Shoo!" said the maiden. "Don't eat up all our cabbages, little rabbit!"

"Come, maiden," said the rabbit, "come

sit on my tail and go with me to my
rabbit hutch."

But the maiden would not.

Another day, back came the rabbit, and
ate away at the cabbages, until the woman
said to her daughter, "Go into the garden,
and drive away the rabbit."

"Shoo! Shoo!" said the maiden. "Don't
eat up all our cabbages, little rabbit!"

"Come maiden," said the rabbit, "come
sit on my tail and go with me to my
rabbit hutch."

But the maiden would not.

Again, a third time back came the rabbit,
and ate away at the cabbages, until the
woman said to her daughter, "Go into the
garden, and drive away the rabbit."

"Shoo! Shoo!" said the maiden. "Don't eat up all our cabbages, little rabbit!"

"Come, maiden," said the rabbit, "come sit on my tail and go with me to my rabbit hutch." And then the girl seated herself on the rabbit's tail, and the rabbit took her to his hutch.

"Now," said he, "set to work and cook some bran and cabbage. I am going to find the wedding guests." And

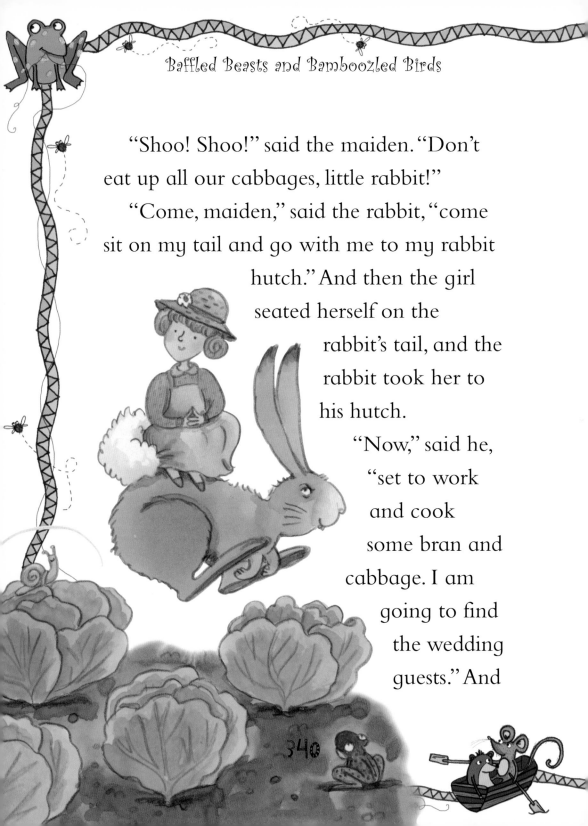

340

soon they were all collected. All the hares
came, and the crow who was to be the
parson to marry them, and the fox for the
clerk, and the altar was under the rainbow.

But the maiden was sad because she was
so lonely.

"Get up! Get up!" said the rabbit. "The
wedding folk are all merry."

But the bride wept and said nothing, and
the rabbit went away, but very soon came
back again. "Get up! Get up!" said he. "The
wedding folk are waiting."

But the bride said nothing, and the
rabbit went away.

Then she made a figure of straw, and
dressed it in her own clothes, and gave it a
red mouth, and set it to watch the kettle of

bran. Then she went home to her mother.

Back again came the rabbit, saying, "Get up! Get up!" and he went up and hit the straw figure on the head, so that it tumbled down.

The rabbit thought that he had killed his bride, and he went away and was very sad.

The Cat and the Mouse

By Joseph Jacobs

The cat and the mouse played together in the malthouse.

The cat bit the mouse's tail off. "Pray, puss, give me my tail," begged the mouse.

"No," said the cat, "I'll not give you your tail, till you go to the cow and fetch me some milk."

First the mouse leaped and then she ran, till she came to the cow, and thus began:

"Pray, cow, give me milk, that I may give cat milk, that cat may give me my own tail again."

"No," said the cow, "I will give you no milk, till you go to the farmer and get me some hay."

First the mouse leaped, and then she ran, till she came to the farmer and thus began:

"Pray, farmer, give me hay, that I may give cow hay, that cow may give me milk, that I may give cat milk, that cat may give me my own tail again."

"No," said the farmer, "I'll give you no hay, till you go to the butcher and fetch me some meat."

The Cat and the Mouse

First the mouse leaped, and then she ran, till she came to the butcher, and thus began:

"Pray, butcher, give me meat, that I may give farmer meat, that farmer may give me hay, that I may give cow hay, that cow may give me milk, that I may give cat milk, that cat may give me my own tail again."

"No," said the butcher, "I'll give you no meat, till you go to the baker and fetch me some bread."

First the mouse leaped and then she ran, till she came to the baker, and thus began:

"Pray, baker, give me bread, that I may give butcher bread, that butcher may give me meat, that I may give farmer meat, that farmer may give me hay, that I may give cow hay, that cow may give me milk, that I

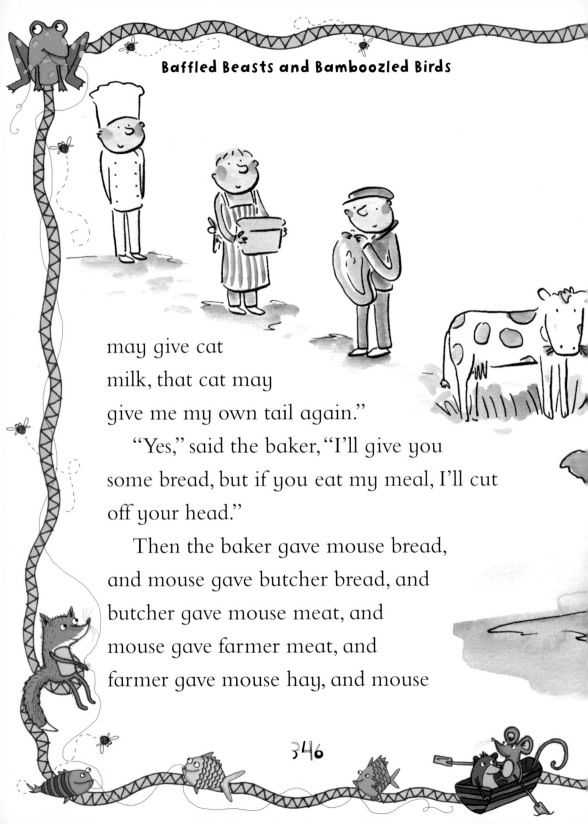

may give cat
milk, that cat may
give me my own tail again."

"Yes," said the baker, "I'll give you
some bread, but if you eat my meal, I'll cut
off your head."

Then the baker gave mouse bread,
and mouse gave butcher bread, and
butcher gave mouse meat, and
mouse gave farmer meat, and
farmer gave mouse hay, and mouse

gave cow hay, and cow gave mouse milk,
and mouse gave cat milk, and cat gave
mouse her own tail again!

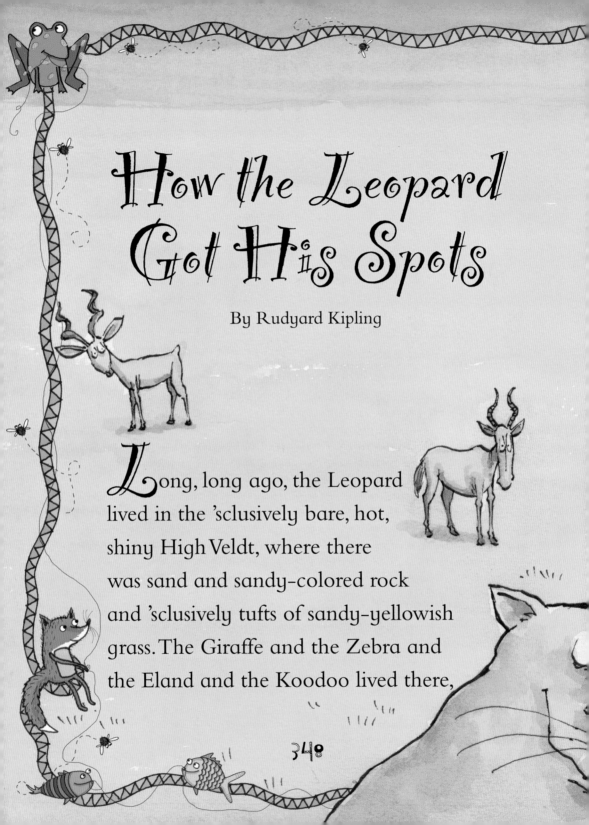

How the Leopard Got His Spots

By Rudyard Kipling

Long, long ago, the Leopard
lived in the 'sclusively bare, hot,
shiny High Veldt, where there
was sand and sandy-colored rock
and 'sclusively tufts of sandy-yellowish
grass. The Giraffe and the Zebra and
the Eland and the Koodoo lived there,

shade and half out of it, and what with the slippery-slidy shadows falling on them, the Giraffe grew blotchy, and the Zebra grew stripy, and the Eland and the Koodoo grew darker, with little wavy gray lines on their backs like bark on a tree trunk. And so, though you could hear them and smell them, you could very seldom see them.

They had a beautiful time in the 'sclusively speckly-spickly shadows of the forest. Meanwhile the Leopard and the Ethiopian ran about over the 'sclusively grayish-yellowish-reddish High Veldt outside, wondering where their breakfasts and their dinners and their teas had gone.

At last they were so hungry that they ate rats and beetles and rock-rabbits, and then they both had the big tummy-ache. Then they met Baviaan, the barking Baboon, who is the wisest animal in All South Africa.

Said Leopard to Baviaan, "Where has all the game gone?"

Said Baviaan, "The game has gone into other spots. My advice to you, Leopard, is to go into other spots too. My advice to you, Ethiopian, is to change as soon as you can."

That puzzled the Leopard and the Ethiopian, but they set off to look. After ever so many days

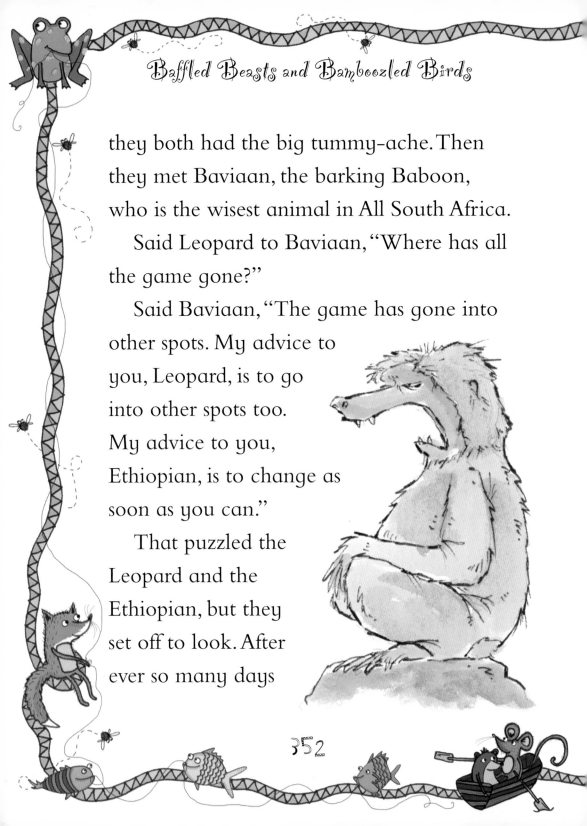

they saw a great, high forest full of tree
trunks all 'sclusively speckled and sprottled
and spottled, dotted and splashed and
slashed and hatched with shadows.

"What is this," said the Leopard, "that is
so 'sclusively dark, and yet so full of little
pieces of light?"

"I don't know," said the Ethiopian, "but I
can smell Giraffe, and I can hear Giraffe,
but I can't see Giraffe."

"That's curious," said the Leopard. "I can
smell Zebra, and I can hear Zebra, but I
can't see Zebra," said the Leopard.

"Wait a bit," said the Ethiopian. "It's a
long time since we've hunted 'em. Perhaps
we've forgotten what they were like."

"Fiddle!" said the Leopard. "I remember

them perfectly on the High Veldt. Giraffe is about seventeen feet high, of a 'sclusively golden-yellow from head to heel. Zebra is about four and a half feet, of a 'sclusively gray-fawn colour from head to heel."

"Then they ought to show up in this dark place like ripe bananas in a smokehouse," said the Ethiopian, looking into the speckly-spickly shadows.

But they didn't. The Leopard and the Ethiopian hunted all day, and though they could smell them and hear them, they never saw one of them.

"For goodness sake," said the Leopard at tea time, "let us wait till it gets dark."

So they waited till dark, and then the Leopard heard something breathing sniffily in the starlight that fell all stripy through the branches. It smelled like Zebra, and it felt like Zebra, and when he knocked it down it kicked like Zebra, but he couldn't see it. So he said, "Be quiet, O you without any form. I am going to sit on your head till morning, because there is something about you that I don't understand."

Presently he heard a grunt and a crash, and the Ethiopian called out, "I've caught a thing I can't see. It smells like Giraffe, and it kicks like Giraffe, but it hasn't any form."

"Sit on its head till morning," said the Leopard. "They haven't any form."

So they sat on them hard till morning time, and then Leopard said, "What have you at your end of the table, Brother?"

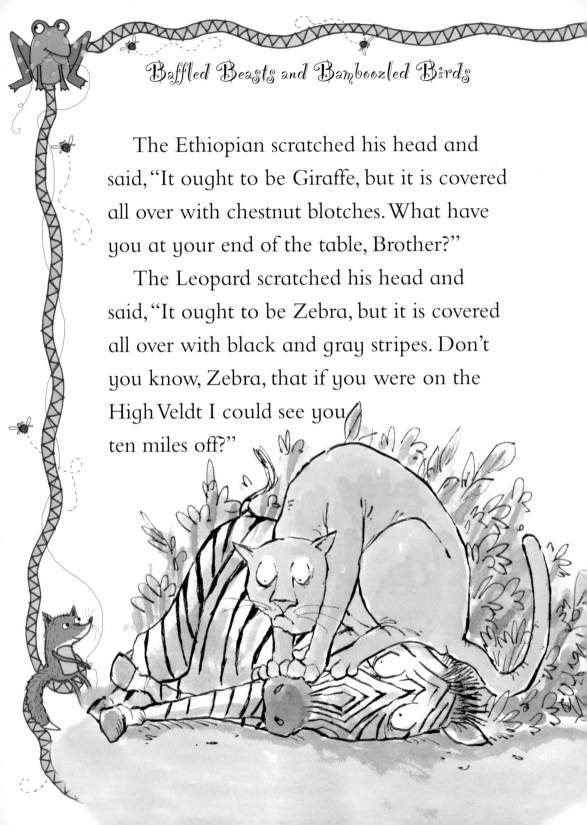

The Ethiopian scratched his head and said, "It ought to be Giraffe, but it is covered all over with chestnut blotches. What have you at your end of the table, Brother?"

The Leopard scratched his head and said, "It ought to be Zebra, but it is covered all over with black and gray stripes. Don't you know, Zebra, that if you were on the High Veldt I could see you ten miles off?"

"Yes," said the Zebra, "but this isn't the High Veldt. Can't you see, Leopard?"

"I can now," said the Leopard. "But I couldn't all yesterday. How is it done?"

"We will show you," said the Zebra.

They let the Zebra and the Giraffe get up. Zebra moved to some thorn bushes where the sunlight fell all stripy, and Giraffe moved to some tallish trees where the shadows fell all blotchy. "Watch," said Zebra and Giraffe. "This is how it's done. One—two—three! Where's your breakfast?"

Leopard stared, and Ethiopian stared, but all they could see were stripy and blotched shadows, no sign of Zebra and Giraffe. They were hidden in the shadowy forest.

"Hi! Hi!" said the Leopard. "That's a

trick worth learning."

"The long and the little of it is that we don't match our backgrounds," said the Ethiopian. "Baviaan's told me I ought to change, and as I've nothing to change except my skin, I'm going to change that."

"What to?" said the Leopard.

"To a nice blackish-brownish color, with a little purple, and touches of slaty-blue— the very thing for hiding in hollows."

He changed his skin then and there.

"But what about me?" said the Leopard, when the Ethiopian had worked his last little finger into his fine new black skin.

"You take Baviaan's advice too. He told you to go into spots. I'll make 'em with the tips of my fingers," said the Ethiopian.

"There's plenty of black left on my skin."

"All right," said the Leopard.

Then the Ethiopian put his five fingers close together and pressed them all over the Leopard. Wherever the five fingers touched they left five little black marks, close together. Sometimes the fingers slipped and the marks blurred, but if you look closely at any Leopard now you will see that there are always five spots—off five black fingertips.

"Now you are a beauty!" said the Ethiopian. "You can lie out on the bare ground and look like a heap of pebbles. You can lie out on a leafy branch and look like sunshine sifting through the leaves, and you can lie across a path and look like nothing

in particular. Think of that!
Now come along, we'll see if
we can't get even with Mr One–Two–
Three Where's your Breakfast!"
So they went away and lived happily
ever afterward. That is all.

How Mr. Rabbit Lost His Tail

By Albert Bigelow Paine

"Once upon a time," said Mr. Rabbit at storytime, "a great many great-grandfathers back, my family had long bushy tails like Mr. Squirrel and Mr. Fox, only a good deal longer and softer, and very handsome."

When Mr. Rabbit said that, Mr. Squirrel sniffed and twitched his nose and gave his nice bushy tail a flirt, but he didn't say anything. Mr. Rabbit went right on.

"Well, there was one fine rabbit who had the longest and plumiest tail of any of the family and was very proud of it. He was my twenty-seventh great-grandfather and was called Mr. Hare. He was young and smart then, and thought he was a good deal smarter than he really was, though he was smart and handsome enough to set the style for all the other rabbits. What's more, he could beat anything running that there was in the Big Deep Woods.

"That twenty-seventh great-grandfather of mine was very proud of his running, and used to brag that in a foot race he could beat anything that lived between the Wide

Grass Lands and the edge of the world. He used to talk about it to almost everybody that came along. One day he met one of the Turtle family, who used to be called Mr. Tortoise in those days. He stopped and began to brag to Mr. Tortoise how fast he could run and how nobody in the Big Deep Woods dared to race with him.

"But Mr. Tortoise just said, 'You can't run very fast. I believe I can beat you myself!'

"Well, that did make Grandpaw Hare laugh—and made him a little mad, too. 'You!' he said. 'Why, I'll give you within ten yards of that rail fence half a mile away, and then beat you across it. Just travel along, and some time this afternoon when you get down that way, I'll come back and let you see me go by. But you'll have to look quick, for I'll be going fast.'

"But Mr. Tortoise said he didn't want any start at all, that he was ready to begin the race right then. That made Grandpaw Hare laugh so loud that Mr. Fox heard him as he was passing, and came over to see what the fun was. Mr. Fox said that he hadn't much to do for a few minutes, and that he'd stay and act as judge. He thought the race wouldn't last long—and it didn't, though it wasn't at all the race he had expected.

"Well, he put Mr. Tortoise and my twenty-seventh great-grandfather side by side, and then he stood off and said, 'Go!' He thought it would be over in a minute.

"Grandpaw Hare gave one great big

leap, about twenty feet long, and then stopped. He wanted to have some fun. He looked around to where Mr. Tortoise was coming straddling and panting along, and he laughed and rolled over to see how solemn he looked. Mr. Tortoise was down on all fours so he could use all his legs at once, and anybody would think, to look at him, that he really expected to win the race. "The more my Grandpaw Hare looked at him the more he laughed.

365

Then he would make another leap forward and stop, look back, and wait for Mr. Tortoise to catch up again.

"Then he would call to him, or maybe go back, and say, 'Come along there, old tobacco box. Are you tied to something?' Mr. Fox would laugh a good deal, too, and he told my ancestor to go on and finish the race—that he couldn't wait around there all day. Pretty soon Mr. Fox said if they were going to fool along like that, he'd just go down to the fence and take a nap till they got there. He told Grandpaw Hare to call to him when he really started to come, so he could wake up and judge the finish.

"Mr. Fox loped away to the fence, and laid down and went to sleep in the shade.

Grandpaw Hare thought it would be fun to pretend to be asleep, too. I've heard a story told about it that says that he really did go to sleep, and that Mr. Tortoise went by him and got to the fence before he woke up. But that is not the way it happened. My twenty-seventh great-grandfather was too smart to go to sleep, and even if he had gone to sleep, Mr. Tortoise made enough noise pawing and scratching along to wake up forty of our family.

"My ancestor would wait until Mr. Tortoise came along and was up even with him, then suddenly he'd sit up as if he'd been waked out of a nice dream and say, 'Hello! What do you want to wake me up for when I'm trying to get a nap?' Then he would laugh and make another big leap, and lie down and pretend again, with his fine plumy tail very handsome in the sun.

"But Grandpaw Hare carried the joke a little too far. He kept letting Mr. Tortoise get up a little closer and closer every time, until Mr. Tortoise would almost step on him before he would move. And that was just what Mr. Tortoise wanted, for the next time he came along he came right up behind my ancestor. Instead of stepping on him, Mr. Tortoise gave his head a quick snap, just as if he were catching fish. He grabbed my Grandpaw Hare by that beautiful plumy tail, and held on. My ancestor gave a squeal and a holler, and set out for that rail fence, telling his troubles as he came.

"Mr. Fox had gone sound asleep and didn't hear the rumpus at first. When he did he thought Grandpaw was just calling to him to wake up and be ready to judge the race, so he sat up quick and watched them come. He saw my ancestor sailing along, with something that looked like an old rusty washpan tied to his tail.

"When Mr. Fox saw what it was, he just laid down, and laughed, and rolled over, and then hopped up on the top rail and called out, 'All right,

I'm awake! Come right along, Mr. Hare.
Come right along! You'll beat him yet!'

"Then Mr. Fox saw my ancestor stop
and shake himself and roll over, to try to get
Mr. Tortoise loose. This of course he couldn't
do, for, as we all know, whenever any of the
Turtle family get a grip they never let go till
it thunders, and this was a bright day. So
pretty soon Grandpaw was up and running
again, with Mr. Tortoise sailing out behind.
Mr. Fox laughed to see them coming, and
called out, 'Come right along, Mr. Hare!
Come right along! You'll beat him yet!'

"But Mr. Fox made a mistake about that.
Grandpaw Hare was really ahead, of
course, when he came down the home
stretch, but when he got close to the fence

he made one more try to get Mr. Tortoise loose. He gave himself and his tail a great big swing. But Mr. Tortoise didn't let go quite quick enough, and off came my twenty-seventh great-grandfather's beautiful plumy tail, and away went Mr. Tortoise with it, clear over the top rail of the fence, and landed in a brier patch on the other side.

"Well, Grandpaw Hare was in such a state as you never heard of! He forgot all about the race at first, and just raved about his loss. He said that he never in the world could show his face before folks again.

"Mr. Fox stopped laughing as soon as he could, and was really quite sorry for him. Even Mr. Tortoise looked through the fence, and asked him if he didn't think it could be spliced and be almost as good as ever.

"He said he hadn't meant to commit any injury, and that he hoped Mr. Hare would live to forgive him, and there was no reason grandpaw shouldn't beat him in race.

"Then my ancestor remembered about the race and forgot his other loss for a minute. He declared that Mr. Tortoise didn't win the race at all—that he couldn't have covered that much ground in half a day alone. He asked Mr. Fox if he was going to let that straddle bug ruin his reputation for speed and make him a laughing stock, besides all the other damage he had done.

"Then Mr. Fox scratched his head, and thought. He said he didn't see how he could help giving the race to Mr. Tortoise, for it was to be the first one across the fence, and Mr. Tortoise was certainly the first one across, and he'd gone over the rail in style.

"Well, that made Grandpaw Hare madder than ever. He didn't say another

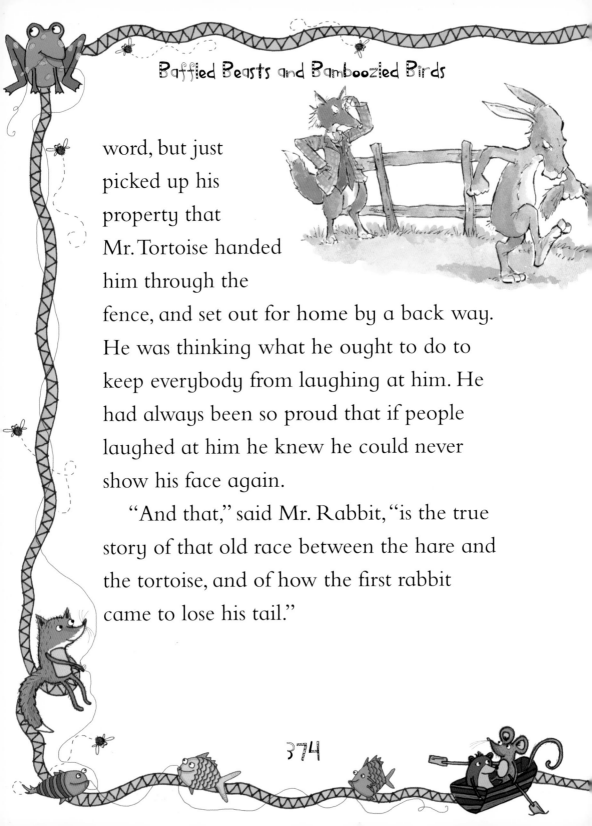

word, but just picked up his property that Mr. Tortoise handed him through the fence, and set out for home by a back way. He was thinking what he ought to do to keep everybody from laughing at him. He had always been so proud that if people laughed at him he knew he could never show his face again.

"And that," said Mr. Rabbit, "is the true story of that old race between the hare and the tortoise, and of how the first rabbit came to lose his tail."

The Hare-Brained Crocodiles

An extract from *The White Hare and the Crocodiles*
by Yei Theodora Ozaki

Long, long ago, when all the animals could talk, there lived in the province of Inaba in Japan, a little white hare. His home was on the island of Oki, and just across the sea was the mainland of Inaba.

Now the hare was bored with life on the tiny island of Oki and wanted very much to cross over to Inaba, where he had heard there were all sorts of new sights to be seen and adventures to be had. Day after day he would go out and sit on the shore and look longingly over the water in the direction of Inaba, and day after day he hoped to find some way of getting across.

One day as usual, the hare was standing on the beach, looking toward the mainland across the water, when he saw a great crocodile swimming near the island.

'This is lucky!' thought the hare. 'Now I shall be able to get my wish. I will ask the crocodile to carry me across the sea!'

But the hare knew that crocodiles were grumpy and unhelpful—not to mention dangerous—and he was doubtful whether the crocodile would agree to do what wanted. So he thought that instead of asking a favor he would try to get what he wanted by a trick.

So with a loud voice he called to the crocodile, and said, "Oh, Mr. Crocodile, isn't it a lovely day?"

The crocodile had come out all by himself that day to enjoy the bright sunshine. Fortunately for the hare, he was just beginning to feel a bit lonely when the hare's cheerful greeting broke the silence. The crocodile swam nearer the shore, very pleased to hear someone speak.

"I wonder who it was that spoke to me just now! Was it you, Mr. Hare? You must be very lonely all by yourself!"

"Oh, no, I am not at all lonely," said the hare, "but as it was such a fine day I came out here to enjoy myself. Won't you stop and play with me a little while?"

The bored crocodile was delighted at the suggestion. He came out of the sea and sat on the shore, and the two played together for some time. Then the hare said, "Mr. Crocodile, you live in the sea and I live on this island, and we do not often meet, so I know very little about you. Tell me, do you think the number of your company is greater than mine?"

"Of course, there are more crocodiles than hares," answered the crocodile haughtily. "Can you not see that for yourself? You live on this small

The Hare-Brained Crocodiles

island, while I live in the sea, which spreads through all parts of the world. If I call together all the crocodiles who dwell in the sea, you hares will be as nothing compared to us!" The crocodile was very conceited.

The hare, who meant to play a trick on the crocodile, said, "Do you think it possible for you to call up enough crocodiles to form a line from this island across the sea to Inaba?"

The crocodile snorted and answered at once, "Of course it is possible."

"Then do try," said the artful hare, "and I will count the number from here!"

The crocodile was very simple-minded. He hadn't the least idea that the hare intended to play a trick on him, so agreed to do what the hare asked, and said, "Wait here a little while I go back into the sea and call all my friends together!"

The crocodile plunged into the sea and was gone for some time. The hare, meanwhile, waited patiently on the shore. At last the crocodile appeared, bringing with him a large number of other crocodiles —they looked like a mass of logs floating on the waves.

"Look, Mr. Hare!" announced the crocodile proudly. "It is nothing for my friends to form a line between here and Inaba. There are enough crocodiles to stretch from here even as far as China or India. Did you ever see so many crocodiles?"

Then the whole company of crocodiles arranged themselves in the water so as to

form a bridge between the Island of Oki
and the mainland of Inaba.

When the hare saw the long, floating
bridge of crocodiles, he said, "How splendid!
I did not believe this was possible. Now let
me count you all! To do this, however, with
your permission, I must walk over you
to the other side, so please be so good as not
to move, or else I shall fall into the sea and
be drowned!"

So the hare hopped off the island on to
the strange bridge of crocodiles, counting as
he jumped from one lumpy, green crocodile

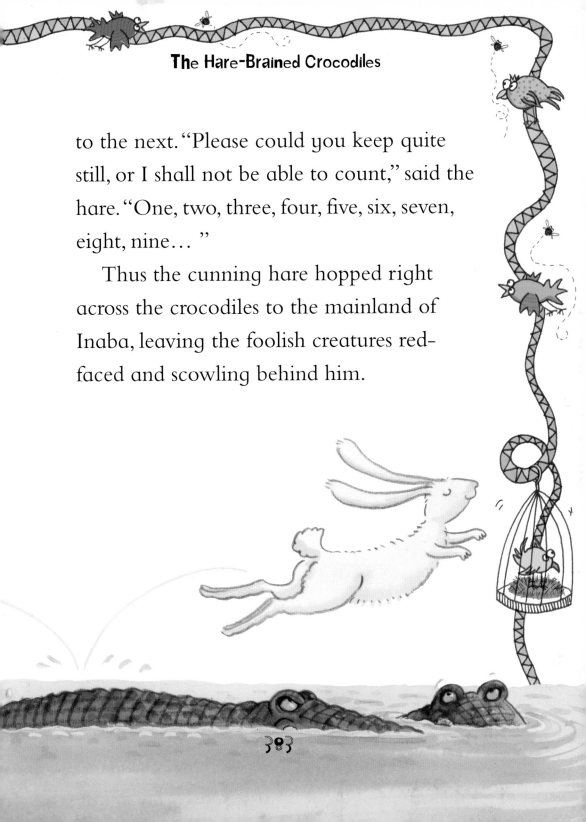

to the next. "Please could you keep quite still, or I shall not be able to count," said the hare. "One, two, three, four, five, six, seven, eight, nine… "

Thus the cunning hare hopped right across the crocodiles to the mainland of Inaba, leaving the foolish creatures red-faced and scowling behind him.

About the Artists

Rosie Brooks Based in London, Rosie has worked as a Cartoonist and Illustrator for nearly a decade, for companies in the UK and abroad. She recently completed an MA in Children's Book Illustration at the Cambridge School of Art and is a regular exhibitor at the Bologna Children's Book Fair.

The Four Little Children Who Went Round the World, A Silly Question, The Field of Boliauns, The Stone Soup, The Moon-Cake, The Hedley Kow, The Cat and the Mouse

Michael Garton After gaining a BA Honors in Illustration in 2004, Michael has been illustrating children's books ever since, for clients including Harper Collins and Hachette. Michael lives and works from his home on the Wirral, UK.

Boots Who Made the Princess Say, "That's a Story", A Most Curious Country, How the Dragon was Tricked, The Greedy Brownie, Mr Vinegar, Day-Dreaming, The Open Road

Jan Lewis Based in Oxfordshire, UK, Jan has been working as an Illustrator since 1978. She has produced work for many British publishers, and BBC children's television. Jan recently gained an MA in Authorial Illustration and now enjoys writing and illustrating her own books for children.

Down the Rabbit-Hole, Master of All Masters, The Endless Tale, Which was the Foolishest?, Wishing for Wings, The Remarkable Rocket, The Simpleton, The Rabbit's Bride, The Hare-Brained Crocodiles

Aimee Mappley After recently achieving a BA Honors in Illustration from Lincoln University, Aimee has shown a keen interest in children's book illustration. She has actively pursued her love of art and design after graduating. This is Aimee's first published work.

Decorative frames

Mike Phillips For the past 15 years Mike has been illustrating children's books, from his home in North Devon, UK. His work has ranged from full-color picture books to the *Horrible Histories* gruesome cartoons.

How the Cow Jumped Over the Moon, The Foolish Weaver, The History of the Seven Families of the Lake Pipple-Popple, The Finest Liar in the World, The Traveling Musicians, The Lad and the Devil, The Three Spinsters, The King's New Turban, The Darning Needle, A Visitor from Paradise, The Blind Men and the Elephant, Why the Bear is Stumpy-Tailed, How the Leopard Got His Spots, How Mr. Rabbit Lost His Tail